The Art of Cheating Episodes: S1E5

The HooKup

EXTENDED AUTHOR'S CUT EDITION

HoLLyRod

COPYRIGHT

Road to Closure
TAOC Prelude
Episode V

April 2012

"Why won't you just tell me where you at, HoLLy?" she probes again, this time with more noticeable frustration in her tone.

"I juss told you where I yam, Carmen," I reply indistinctly without looking away from the road. "I'm onna highway. Driving."

Her voice gets louder through the speaker, "Ok, but on the highway driving *where??* I know yo drunk ass ain't been driving this whole fucking time!!! You slurring yo words n'shit! What the fuck is you on right now, bro?? Like...for real, HoLLy!! Where you going?"

Carmen never raises her voice at me like this without apologizing immediately afterwards, so I pause briefly, off instinct. But it's to no avail. This time, she's not sorry.

"Hello?!?!" she screams at the awkward silence.

"I'm still here," I reply without enthusiasm, fighting my natural urge to yell. She need to lower her damn voice.

"HoLLy. For real...like what the fuck?!? Are you driving back to Saint Louis or sum'n?" she wonders. "Where is Sug at?"

My left eyebrow raises in confusion. It's at this very

moment that I realize Carmen couldn't possibly know every detail about what's going on tonight. Cuz if she *did*, she'd know for a fact that Sug was on her way back to the Lou and that I was chasing her down the highway like a bat outta hell. Ain't no way she'a be asking these stupid ass questions if she knew what was up. No fucking way.

Right?

"It don't e'en matter," I tell her, speeding up to switch lanes. "And ain't nobody even drunk like dat anyway girl! I pulled up on yo ass – cleeerlee I can still drive. Chill tha fuck out, man. Fa real."

"Man, but you took like ten shots when you was here, boo! Like…how the fuck you just gon leave like that? I swear if I wuttin' half-sleep! I'm thinking you going to get some ice n'shit and you done bounced!"

When Carmen spilled the beans to me about Sug earlier…I'll admit, I started to see red. I kept pacing back and forth n'shit, taking shots of *Henny* to the face, cussing up a storm. She tried to calm me down by pulling my dick out to get it wet. And any other time, that shit mighta worked. I couldn't think straight or appreciate her sloppy throat in that moment, even if I wanted to, though. Carmen got some good ass pussy, too – don't get me wrong. But even once we started fucking, I couldn't focus for shit. The whole time she was riding a nigga, bouncing on this **wooD**, I was already picturing myself on the highway – plotting. Totally blindsided at what I had just read, I just got dressed and shook the spot right after Carmen nutted and started dozing off.

"Man," I sigh as the thoughts flash back. "I hadda go, Carmen."

"Go *where*, boo?" she keeps probing. "Did you talk to Sug? Where is she at? I don't understand why you won't just tell me what's going on!! Like…*where are you going*? Are you by yoself? What the fuck, boo???"

Her fussing is making my head hurt. I really don't feel like hearing all this shit right now, let alone explaining myself. This some bullshit. I knew I shouldn't have even fuckin' answered the phone.

"So why the fuck you answer then, nigga? You been bouncing from wall-to-wall like this all damn night! Make up yo mind, HoLLy!"

"Cuz nigga she was blowing me up and you kept threatening to answer n'shit! Tha fuck else was I supposed to do?"

"Nigga, please! We was both sick of her ass calling like that! And all I said was she might have some mo' info for us, but nigga you knew she was gon drill you soon as you answered. Just handle dat shit and quit crying, bro. Got-damn!"

I don't know…I guess I'm just more irritated at the fact that she's so damn confused right now. Earlier when we was in **Carmen's Room** down on Westport, it was me with all the questions and she had all the answers. I mean, not even a couple of fuckin' hours ago, it seemed like Carmen knew exactly what was going on with Sug's betrayal tonight.

"Why you acking like you 'ont know what tha fuck going on, all'a a sudden? You saw dat shit in her diary befo' I did, Carmen – you da one showed me the fuckin' screenshots! Now you playin' dumb n'shit. You 'bout ta piss me tha fuck off, girl."

"Boo, calm down," her voice softens up. "I told you everything I know already. I'm just trying to figure out what *you* on right now. I know you mad as fuck, but you ain't gotta be taking dat shit out on *me*, HoLLy. I'm on yo side."

"Gotdamn right, I'm mad as fuck!" I blurted. "Cuz she got me fucked up, man. Fa real doe."

"Have you talked to her yet? Don't tell her how you found out, HoLLy."

"Man, ain't nobody 'bout to tell her you told me – shut dat shit up, bro. And I ain't e'en talked to her ass yet anyway. Punk ass bitch done turned her fuckin' phone off. She prolly done blocked me wit her stoopid ass."

I must've called Sug like twenty times in the few minutes it took me to jog through the hotel lobby on the way to **MyPrecious**. By the time I was leaving the parking lot, Sug's phone was going straight to voicemail. She ain't know what I had just found out from Carmen though. She was just being the petty bitch that Sug is, ignoring my calls after we fell out earlier.

"Wait, so she don't know you know yet?" Carmen gasps in disbelief. "Boo, tell me what's going on!! Who is *the Italian* she was talking about? Is it who I'm thinking it is?"

"I juss told you I ain't talked ta her ass," I snap back. "And you know who tha fuck the Italian is, Carmen. I really wish you'a stop playin' stupid, bro! Fa real! You know eggzaklee what she on if you juss use sum common fuckin' sense! Damn!"

"I'm not playing stupid though, HoLLy! I'm asking cuz I really don't know! I mean, come on now. I ain't even know you and Sug was *talking* again, let alone y'all was *back in town this weekend!* Shit...last I heard you wuttin' e'en fucking wit her no mo!" she rants in frustration. "Like I said earlier...I just saw yo tweet about *Town Topic*...and I'm like *'I know this nigga ain't snuck in the city without telling me!'* So I just called you to see wassup. That's it. That's all. This is *me*, HoLLy. I'm not playing stupid, boo."

She sounds so convincing. I guess I ain't got no reason to not believe her, though, if I'm being honest. Shit, I done believed her this far along the way. I'm pretty sure Carmen ain't know I was back in KC this weekend with Sug; she had no idea we was on this money mission together. I mean – for real – how could she? How could Carmen have any real clue about the type of night I been having around this bitch?

Shit...even *I'm* still having a hard time accepting how tonight got to this point...

Earlier tonight: 11:48pm

Sug had left our hotel room earlier to go meet up with this trick on the east side and ended up being gone

ix

way longer than I expected. At first, I wuttin' tripping. I figured she was just mad about the heated exchange we had before she left and taking her time on purpose. So I hopped on *Twitter* real quick, and asked my timeline what I should eat for the night: Denny's or Town Topic. I was just shooting the shit – you know – trying to stall out for as long as I could cuz I really didn't even wanna seem like I gave a fuck that Sug wuttin' back yet.

I eventually swallowed my pride after about an hour or so and called her. I mean, I had to at least make sure she was safe – *right?*

The first few attempts – no answer. Then when she finally did decide to pick up – she had an attitude n'shit. Talmbout she was done with me. That turned into another big shouting match before the bitch had the nerve to hang up in my face. I couldn't fumble my phone quick enough trying to call her right back. When she ain't answer, I was like, '*Ion know where the fuck this bitch at, but I betchu I'm 'bout to hop in deez streets and find her ass. She got me fucked up*'. But then soon as I grabbed my keys, my phone started ringing and I softened up – thinking Sug was calling me back to apologize.

Turns out it was Carmen, calling to question me about my tweets and why I ain't tell her I was back in town. She was antsy as fuck, acting like she really needed to see me right away. And I mean – we hadn't linked up in a minute, with me living in St. Louis now n'shit. So, when Carmen told me she had a room down on Westport and asked me to come match a blunt – since I was only minutes away, I packed up the room and said 'fuck it'. Sug was on some bullshit and I started feeling like two can play that game.

But then, after we started smoking, Carmen suddenly remembered she needed to show me these pictures from Sug's diary that she had been 'meaning to tell me about'. She ain't say why, but she'd apparently snuck and read through Sug's personal journal the last time they worked the same party. Or...it could've been one of those times we was all at the *Kweens Kwarters* together. I don't really know for real. Regardless of when it happened though, Carmen probably didn't know what some of that shit on the pages actually meant. That's likely why she waited so long to even bring it up to me.

3:55am

"Bro," I take a deep breath. "I know you rememba the whole shit wit the Italian nigga, *Lorenzo*. The *same* nigga I hooked you up with for yo first trick."

"I remember," she confirms. "The nigga that ran off with our money. What was that...the summer before last?"

"Exactly! Now dat's enuff ta put two-n-two togetha, Carmen. You know what happened wit dat hoe ass nigga, and you seen she still been talking to dat muthafucka! Why the fuck would they still be talking?? At all?!?! *Fuck man!* This whole fucking trip was prolly a setup, on the real!" I pause, thoughts drifting. "*Dawg.* I'ma kill this bitch, bro."

"HoLLy, stop talking like that," she urges. "Calm down, boo."

"Man, *fuck all'at*," I snarl, biting my lip. "You on sum babyback bullshit! You barely sound woke anyway. I'ma juss call you back."

She starts panicking, screaming into the phone again, "No, don't hang up! *HoLLy!* I'm up now, just talk to me."

"Nah, gone take yo ass back ta sleep. I'm cool man. I know what I gotta do."

"What that mean, HoLLy? What are you 'bout to do?!?" she yells.

"Don't worry about it," I mumble, glancing over at the phone and the pistol in the passenger seat.

"Boo, can you just come back to my room? Cuz you talking too fuckin' crazy and you not in yo right mind at all. And plus, I'm horny again anyway. Come back."

"Carmen, I'm haffway to Saint Louis right now. I'm not 'finna turn around. Fuck dat. I'm 'bout ta pull up on dis bitch, and I'm getting my muhfuckin' money back. Fuck her, fuck the Italian, fuck whoeva else she wit. Errbody got me fucked up!" I yell with anger and intensity in my voice.

"But how you even know it's the same Italian, though?" she challenged. "She ain't say Lorenzo's name; she just kept saying *'the Italian'*. So how you know it's him, boo?"

This takes me over the edge, causing me to swerve back into the right lane of the highway. The ~~beast~~ has been fairly quiet in my head since I decided to finally answer Carmen's back-to-back-to-back calling. But I'm not sure how much longer it's gon stay that way though, if she keep talking like this...planting these bullshit seeds of doubt.

"Man what?!" I exclaim loudly. "Are you seerius right now, girl??? Tha fuck you mean?!?! Dawg, you know gotdamn muhfuckin' well it ain't no otha Italian she talkin' about, Carmen! It's the same fuckin' nigga, bro!"

She's not moved one bit. "But boo, how do you *know*?"

"Man, I'm 'bout ta go, girl," I mumble through tight lips, reaching for the phone. "I'll juss talk to you lata."

"No, HoLLy, hold on! I gotta tell you something el..."

"Girl, bye," I end the call before she can finish, immediately putting my EVO on silent before tossing it back in the passenger seat. I've had more than enough of this probing bullshit.

For almost two hours now, I've been on my own trying to figure this whole Sug shit out, putting together the details of her plot. But I'm at least convinced that *Lorenzo* is involved in Sug's plan to snake me. Ain't no other Italian she could be referring to in the diary entries. This much I'm sure of.

Right?

"Nigga you know it's Lorenzo!" my inner beast needs no further convincing. *"Stay focused, HoLLy."*

"Yeah but, hold on, bro. Cuz if it ain't Lorenzo…then that mean we wrong about what Sug is on."

"Nigga. You letting Carmen fuck with yo head right now bruh. What other Italian do we even know? Come on, dawg."

"I mean. What about **Richie***?"*

"Richie?!?" the beast screams in my head. *"Richie-fuckin-Morelli? You fucking with me, right?!? Nigga that was Sashé's trick! Why the fuck would Richie Morelli's square ass be tryna help Sug get this bullshit off tonight?"*

"Man I don't know — I ain't thought it thew dat far yet. But I'm saying…hear me out though. Richie **is** *Italian,"* I try to justify my newfound and slightly reasonable doubt.

"Stop fucking playing, HoLLy. We ain't crossed paths with Richie in years. Richie never even knew you existed, nigga. Carmen got you bugging — it's simple as that."

"Man fuck, bro!" I pounded the steering wheel with my fist. *"I don't even know what fuckin' make sense now, bro! You might be right. Maybe Richie ain't the Italian. But this is* **Sug** *we talmbout, too. We can't put nuttin' past her, bro. You know dat shit."*

"True dat, muhfucka. Cuz I BEEN saying dat. But check it — you just said a minute ago — if it ain't Lorenzo she referring to in the diary,

then it ain't a setup like we thought. Right?"

"Right! That's all I'm saying!"

"But you read dat shit yoself bro. You saw her talking about 'plotting with the Italian behind HoLLy's back'. So we know, just based off of that statement, Sug is plotting, nigga. At the very least we know she on some snake shit. And it makes perfect sense for it to be Lorenzo hoe ass helping her."

*"It makes perfect sense to **assume** it's him…yeah,"* I'm still having second thoughts. *"Cuz what if, for some reason, it's **not** Lorenzo?"*

"Man nah, HoLLy, come on bro. Just think about it. Sug set everything up this weekend, dawg. This trip was all her idea. Us working Marshall's party together – her idea. Plus…who set up the deal at the after-party with Marshall's so-called old 'friend' who was looking for them pills? Yeah nigga – Sug! It all leads back to her, bruh. And then the icing on the cake – how did we even meet that lame, Italian nigga in the first place, HoLLy? Through OG Marshall – that's how. Renzo is OG's boy. And both of them old ass niggas was two of Sug's biggest tricks. Come on, dawg. Renzo is the Italian. It ain't rocket science!"

"Yeah but, remember OG fell out with Lorenzo over that money that came up missing too," I continue to remind myself. *"Marshall took a L just like we did – he ain't been fucking with Lorenzo since 2010, bro, when all'at shit happened. And I doubt Renzo even know that nigga that bought the pills the other night."*

"Allegedly," the **beast** whispers. *"For all we know, the pill nigga was Renzo's boy too! And every one of dem hoe ass niggas coulda been in on that lick two years ago, bro. Can't put shit past Sug – remember?"*

"Man...fuck nah, bro," I shake my head. *"Renzo snaked errbody dat night — me, OG Marshall, Sug, the other dancers. All of us nigga! Ain't no way Marshall was in on dat. You don't remember dat nigga OG was helping us look for dat salami eating ass nigga? Dat nigga was shooting at the Italian's house wit us, bro. I know you 'memba dat shit."*

"Aww yeah, ok, that's right. Ok. I'll give you dat. Maybe Marshall didn't help Renzo rob us back when all'at shit went down. Maybe. But that don't mean Sug didn't. If dat bitch still been talking to the Italian this whole time, ain't no telling how far back her plotting goes. You know dat, HoLLy. That robbery coulda easily been another one of her clever ideas. Da bitch stay full of 'em."

The ~~beast~~ makes a good point talking about Sug and her sneaky, clever ideas. It's just super hard for me to believe that she woulda helped Lorenzo run off with everybody's money when he robbed us a couple years back. Nah man...cuz she was pissed off. And the two of us went on more than a couple revenge-filled missions trying to hit the Italian where it hurt.

But at any rate, the ~~beast~~ is partially right, at least about *tonight*. I did see with my own eyes that Sug been talking to the Italian again long after he robbed us, plotting tonight's grand scheme with this nigga behind my back.

HoLLy would kill me if he knew it was the Italian helping me with all of this. I wish I could see the look on his face when he finds out... "

When I read her stinging words earlier tonight, I

xvi

immediately assumed it was a reference to *Lorenzo the Italian*. Knowing Renzo had robbed us before, it just made too much sense that he was '*the Italian*' in question. But that was before Carmen just pointed out that Sug never actually said his *name* in her journal. Now I feel like I need to confirm if it's really him.

"*You tripping, nigga.*"

"*How bro?? I'm tryna figure this shit out!*"

"*Ain't shit to figure out! You know it's Renzo, you just love second guessing obvious shit like this.*"

Man bro, you know I fucking hate second-guessing shit!!! Stop patronizing me, nigga."

"*Shit...nigga, I can't tell...*"

"*Maaan just shut up and lemme think dis shit through – just one time my nigga! I'm sick of yo shit!*"

Lorenzo Caruso was this older cat in his mid 40's who we originally met through his former longtime homeboy, a nigga that went by *OG Marshall*. They claimed they met doing time together back in the 90's. Lorenzo supposedly got caught up as part of a sting operation on his family's chop shop business and keeping his mouth shut landed him a 7-year bid. OG, who was a little older, was already serving time for multiple grand theft auto and armed robbery charges when Renzo hit the yard. The two of them formed a strong bond behind bars that led to them working together on the outside after being released.

By the time Sug and I crossed OG's path, he was just this thirsty and damn-near 50-year-old ass nigga who 'knew' a bunch of tricks like himself looking for a good time. During that infamous spring of 2010 when we stepped into the world of sex work, Marshall helped Sug get started by hooking her up with her first party.

You see, for months prior to the moment she decided to start selling actual pussy, OG was one of Sug's original tricks. He was the typical type – you seen him around. One of those older, paid niggaz who loved them younger girls in their early 20's.

Aye I ain't gon front though. I can't really judge dude completely cuz shit – now that I'm 33 – I still prefer 'em around that age myself. But still, this OG nigga was at that point in life where he'a spend ten times more money in the pursuit of pussy than any nigga my age or younger.

OG was a regular at the strip clubs in KC, which is where Sug first met him. I'm still undecided on if I believe Sug's story that she ain't start stripping until after she was my bitch. She be lying so fuckin' much. But anyway, so yeah, I was sitting in the parking lot waiting to take her home that first night she gave OG Marshall her phone number. And I saw the way he looked at her then, walking her to the car drooling n'shit. Soon as we pulled off, I advised her to keep him close. I could just tell this nigga was thirsty and ready to spend some bread for Sug's attention. I mean, the muhfucka texted her like ten times before we even made it back to the *Graham Suites* that night.

The man was clearly giving off serious 'sugar daddy' vibes, but wildly enough, Sug couldn't pick up on the clues and thought I was just talking shit. That's why our conversation on the ride home that night was so fucking pivotal.

I mean she was already working at the strip club. So, I started telling her in the car that she need to figure out how to finesse her customers outta even more cash – starting with OG. Don't get it twisted – Suga B was no stranger to using her sexual appeal as a weapon. But she was hesitant to understand my angle at first. I mean yeah – she already knew she could have any man she wanted. But see at the same time, Sug had never sold sex for money thus far or even received cash directly from the men who chased her.

Damn, that shit felt like a deja vü too, man…like I had been there before.

At this point though, before 2010, I only had minimal experience in this area myself. But after all the shit I'd been through in my previous relationship with Sashé, at this stage in my life, I had at least learned how to benefit financially from having the girl that everybody wanted.

Shay was one of the baddest chicks in in the city and our lifestyle had led us down taboo pathways. Between us chasing ménages and *her* part-time stripping experiment, eventually Sashé ended up in the same rooms with men who paid for eye candy on their arms, way before Suga B was in the picture.

It started off with *Richard Morelli*, the Italian lawyer Shay met working the club one night back in early 2008. Richie was recently divorced and had become a regular at Club Lava prior to Sashé and her bff, Kris, being hired.

After seeing Sashé on the pole for the first time, Richie was instantly infatuated and started only visiting the club on nights she was at work. She was coming home with hundreds of dollars during those days – no exaggeration. Then Richie would eventually ask to see Shay outside of the club and offer to become her sugar daddy, in exchange for escorting him on dates.

When Shay first told me about Richie's proposal back then, I had mixed feelings. I mean, I had already swallowed my pride in being cool with my lady dancing naked for money. And I had to convince myself that the shit was acceptable because of the cash flow, as long as it was just dancing for tips at work. But when Sashé told me we had a trick wanting to take it the extra step, the whole offer rubbed me the wrong way at first. At the time, I didn't know if I could realistically handle the idea of my girl having a sugar daddy on the side. I never felt so conflicted in my whole life.

Sashé was persistent, though. She thought Richie presented a helluva opportunity and she had been with me long enough to know how to drive home a hard bargain.

You see, my relationship with Shay was built on openness and trust…and we were a team. We had rules of our own back then, and she reminded me that if she only used Richie for his money – that it was still within our rules. Shay insisted that she had no intentions on fucking Richie or even letting him think it could go there. She wanted me to simply look the other way while she brought us in more cash. And it was hard not to see where she was coming from for real, especially when she pointed out how she had been looking the other way at all the 'appreciation' some of my 'fans' were showing me at the time. Shay trusted me…and she needed me to trust her – the same way.

With that being said, I reluctantly agreed that Shay could have Richie as her sugar daddy…without giving him any sugar.

Years later though, by the time Sug was around, I was in a much darker space. But at the same time, the place still felt very familiar. OG Marshall immediately struck me as the Richie Morelli type, and this time around, I understood the assignment.

It's crazy how the tables turn…

In the beginning, the situation with Sug was really no different than when I was with Shay. I had a girl who worked as a stripper, and she had clients she would see outside of the club. They would go on dates that would often end with a private dance at the clients' home, but there was no sex involved. In the beginning, the thought of being a prostitute was as repulsive to Sug as it was to Shay, and even myself for that matter. That sugar daddy money was steady enough at first, and we all ate good. In the beginning.

Then the spring of 2010 came around, and Sug and I

found ourselves in that crazy financial bind. This time though, it was Sug with the bright idea of taking it the extra step. After she had been declining OG's continuous offers to pay for sex for months, she believed selling pussy could be the foolproof fix to our money problems. She felt like Marshall would be the perfect first customer, but honestly, Sug never had to work hard to convince me on it. Because deep down...I knew it could work. Deep down inside...I *wanted* it to work.

I was in a much darker space by then...

Remember, when I met Sug, I was out for blood. Bitter and jaded from how Sashé walked out on me...and looking for revenge. I knew I wasn't supposed to fall for Sug...I knew my inner ~~beast~~ was furious about it. This girl was a stripper and a scammer for crying out loud. I tried to ignore all the scrutiny from my subconscious...but deep down inside, I knew he was right. I had no business falling for a girl like Sug in the first place, so when I took it a step further and went with Sug's money chasing plan, it was like I was trying to save face with the ~~beast~~.

"Don't put that all on me, nigga. It was a foolproof idea and the best move. You the one who went off course and got in ya feelings with dat bitch."

"Man, you know what I'm tryna say...you saw dollar signs and agreed with taking the extra step," I quip back. *"Like you always do."*

"Nigga, you just explained to yourself how YOU wanted Sug to sell pussy! You literally just said it was you who talked her into finessing

xxii

niggas...the same way you convinced Sashé to do the shit!"

"Man whatever! I ain't convince Shay – she brought dat sugar daddy shit to me! I gave Shay permission...that's not the same thing!"

"Same fucking difference, nigga – you know what I'm saying. Don't put none of that on me – blame yourself nigga."

"Blaming you is blaming a part of myself, hoe ass nigga – let's not get it twisted! I wouldn't have done half this shit without you! Couldn't have!"

"But a hour ago...you just said you did! Remember The Hangover episode, right? Yeah nigga. Keep that same energy!"

"Man nah, hold up dawg...you tryna switch shit around! I only brought up Hangover cuz you was talking dat shit like I needed you to **cheat**!! No nigga! Stop fucking playing with me! Cuz I never, not once said I was a angel before I could hear yo voice. I already admitted I found The Art on my own! I'm talmbout all this extra shit you be having a nigga on – beyond the cheating! Fuck outta here! You know what the fuck I'm saying – you tryna change the subject."

"Nigga, you tryna change the subject – I thought we was talking about who the Italian is anyway!"

"Aww yeah – see what I'm saying?! You keep making me lose my train of thought, nigga! Shut the fuck up so I can hear myself think! Damn. Now where was I?"

About two weeks after Sug turned her first trick, OG Marshall sent her another client who he claimed was his longtime partner-in-crime – the half-Black, half-Italian nigga they called Renzo. From the moment I met him, Lorenzo came off as the shady type. But he and OG spent so much bread on pussy through the spring and summer, I just constantly shrugged off his bad energy. That proved to be a mistake the infamous night the Italian ran off with all of our cash from this after-hours gig he booked us for.

From that moment on, Lorenzo was considered public enemy #1 to the *Kweens Kwarters*. We spent the next couple of months searching high and low, but that muhfucka was gone in the wind. Sug even put a bounty out on him, offering cash payment to any local hoes willing to give up intel on where he might be hiding out. She wanted to kill that nigga…and I can't say I ever tried to talk her out of it. We lost big time that night, especially since I still paid Carmen and the other girls their base pay for showing up. And the way Sug and I started falling out of sync after that robbery made me want to see Lorenzo truly suffer a slow death.

Luckily, we never saw the nigga again. The search got called off by default when we left Kansas City and the pussy-selling hustle behind, but the hatred for the Italian never died down between me and Sug. At least I *thought* so…until I saw her diary tonight.

"So, you do admit that the Italian is Lorenzo then! Ok, great! Now can we stop bullshitting and get back to focusing on catching dis bitch?"

"We still don't 100% know it's him yet! Carmen is right, bro. Sug ain't never say his name."

"Man dat's bullshit, HoLLy! I promise you overthinking dis shit! Look

at the screenshots again, nigga!"

"*The screensho…aww yeaaa – dat's right! Carmen did send me the pics!"*

Suddenly I'm reminded that Carmen sent the evidence to my phone before we started fucking tonight. I don't know how I forgot about that shit that quick.

"Yea…like I said. What would you do without me?"

I ignore the banter from the beast and attempt to reach for my phone again without losing my grip on the steering wheel. The shit is harder than it sounds…cuz two seconds later, I'm swerving on the shoulder again.

Oh fuckin' well.

I could care less about getting stopped by police right now. I gotta take a look at these pics again.

"*Cuz nigga, I know I ain't tripping! I know what the fuck that bitch said. You got me fucked up, bro. Where dat shit at?"* I mumble to myself, holding my EVO up near the windshield. "*Damn – it's 4 o'clock already?!? Fuck!!!"*

The battery on my phone is under 50% now, cuz Carmen ain't stopped calling since I hung up on her and she keep sending me texts. I scroll past all of that, opening up my photos folder. As soon as I click on the first picture, I lose my grip on the device…and it bounces against the dashboard and gear shift before falling to the passenger-side floor.

"Gotdammit man! See what you made me do, nigga?! Talkin' bout 'I need you'! Stupid shit man!!!"

"You need me to get the phone for yo clumsy ass now, nigga?"

"Man, yeah right! Go 'head, lemme see you try then, nigga!"

"Nah, you good. You 'Superman'. You got it, playboy."

"Yeah, that's what thought!" I snap back at myself as I start pumping the brakes and pulling the car over in frustration. *"You just talkin' shit – like always, nigga. That's all you ever do."*

"See, that's yo problem. You don't know how to be real wit yoself about what I really do for us."

"Nigga what is it dat you do besides help me outta situations you got us caught up in? Like tonight?" I look in the rearview and turn my hazard lights on.

"Correction nigga – YOU get us in deez jams cuz you pick and choose when to listen to me. I told you not to fall for Sug. And it took you seeing her diary for yoself before you admitted I was right about dat bitch!"

"So what, nigga??" I take the seatbelt off, gathering myself. *"You acting like YOU showed me the bitch diary! Nigga that wuttin' you – that was Carmen!"*

"Yeah, but nigga who made sure you kept Carmen close? Yo dumb ass really tried to cut off contact wit her just to make up with Sug! You tried that same bullshit after KeLLy's Revenge with Cookie, nigga. On all bullshit."

"*Cookie?*" my face turns up as I reach around the floor for my phone. "*What the fuck Cookie gotta do with Carmen, nigga? What are we even talking about right now?!*"

"*Gotdamn HoLLy!! I gotta spell everything out for you, my nigga?!? You can't even keep up wit ya own thoughts no more!*"

"*Man whatever, cuzz,*" I bite my lip. "*Lemme look through deez pics so we can get back on the road.*"

"*I'm saying – think about it, HoLLy. You said the deja vü was about KeLLy's Revenge. You found out Kells was plotting from Cookie, nigga. Yo main side chick! The same way you just found out about Sug from Carmen, genius! Connect the fuckin' dots, nigga!*"

"*Yeah, but Carmen ain't really my side chick.*"

"*She might as well be, HoLLy! We both know how the Son's Curse works but you seem to forgot how to fuckin' listen to it! You know the rules, nigga! Always keep a roster, nigga! Always keep 'em fighting for that top spot, nigga! I kept you on yo toes when you wanted to get rid of Cookie and I kept you on yo toes when you tried to cut off Carmen and all the rest of 'em! You need me, nigga. Just like you needed every one of deez hoes in yo stable over the years. The Art of Cheating is the art of cheating, homie.*"

"*So you tryna say...the Warrensburg sign flashback...is about Carmen tipping me off like Cookie did?*"

"*I'm saying you all over the place for no reason, dawg. The shit is right in yo face! You flashing back to Sassy and all dis other shit – overthinking it.*"

"*Man, I only thought about Sassy cuz when I relapsed, that's the first time I heard yo voice. Damn, how dis shit slide way under the fuckin' seat??"* I finally pull the phone out and start immediately scrolling.

"I mean...but dat wuttin' the first time, HoLLy. If we being technical."

I sighed in frustration, *"Man stop dat shit, bro. I'm talmbout the first time I could hear you loud and clearly."*

"Yeah nigga, and I'm saying that was way before you relapsed wit Sassy!"

"Bruh, I'm not doing dis wit you!"

"Damn HoLLy. You really don't remember huh? You getting old."

"Nigga ain't shit wrong wit my memory! You been around for a minute but you wuttin' never strong enough to have a voice 'til Sassy!"

"I mean nigga, I get why you don't remember. You was still tripping off Kells cheating — feeling guilty about Cookie. You was out of it in dat moment...and needed me to take over."

"Man, you smokin' werk, bro," I wave him off. *"I ain't never blacked out like dat!"*

"Unless you did..."

"When nigga?"

"Bruh, how the fuck do you not remember Tianna? The restraints? The candlewax?"

I pause, staring right through my phone screen, *"Tianna? The bitch I got hooked up with after KeLLy's Revenge?"*

"Right — but Tianna wuttin' just some random bitch you linked up with after that night, nigga. You was following the rules, HoLLy. You had to rebuild ya roster after all'at shit wit Kells."

"Ok I ain't gon argue what I was on wit da roster. And nigga I just thought about Tee last week when we fucked Lisa — so nigga, I ain't forgot shit! But I know you ain't tryna say you was in my ear with Tianna, bruh. You got Tee confused with Sassy. Tianna was was a whole year before Sassy!"

"Nah, you got it confused, HoLLyRod! And you don't remember cuz you got triggered and blacked out. And I had to take over."

"Bro, you wuttin' **talking** *den. I wuttin' talking to* **myself** *like dis den! I would remember dat shit. I remember yo energy got stronger after KeLLy's Revenge when Tianna tried that Dom shit…but dawg, you wuttin' TALKING talking 'til Sassy was talkin' dat ménage shit."*

"Ok. Put the phone on the charger then, big dawg. Turn the recorder on…and just keep retracing yo steps like you said, HoLLy. So, what happened after KeLLy's Revenge?"

At that moment, something sparked in my head and I swallowed with a big gulp.

"Wait…hold up. Maybe you right, bro…"

*   *   *   *   *

…to be continued in TAOC Episodes S1E5

Have you ever seen a picture or a portrait –
full of beautiful color and intricate detail, so
complex and deep, and exploding with pure
artistry???? Give it but a glance and you'll never
appreciate the true brilliance behind it.
Yet…stare at it for too long.…and you'll
become consumed by its mystique and engrossed
to near obsession.

Cheating is a work of art.

This…

…is the masterpiece that I've always liked to
call…

The Art of Cheating

1

April 2004

I shoulda known this *hooKup* was a bad idea from the jump! More times than not, *hookups* just don't work out. I mean think about it – the very idea of somebody playing matchmaker is some overrated shit!! One of these days I've gotta stop thinking with my dick…

"Naw nigga…I ain't crazy!" Tianna screamed into the phone. "I know what I just heard!" Her voice was high-pitched, and she was mad as fuck.

This dat bullshit!!!

"Girl, I don't know what the hell you talking about," I tried to sound serious.

"So why it take you so long to answer?" she shot back. "*And* I called you twice!"

"Maaan I just said my phone was in the other room girl! You tripping…for real dude."

"No, I'm not!!!" she barked. "Just be real, Rodney! You telling me you don't know who I'm talking about?"

"I have no idea," I replied confidently.

"You lying!!!" Tianna snapped in frustration. "Oh my *God* – *both* of y'all are some *liars!!!!* I swear…niggaz ain't about shit!!!"

I started getting antsy, looking for a way out, "Man ain't nobody got time for this shit man. I'm 'bout to hang up on you."

"You better not fucking hang up on me, nigga! I swear to *God* – don't hang up on me, boy! You caught – just man up and admit it!"

I exhaled in frustration, shaking my head. This bitch is really tripping. I can tell she not gonna let this shit go. Maybe it's time to just cut her loose…cut our ties now before it gets too outta hand. Sometimes you gotta know when to fold them, and the way Tianna is going off in my ear right at this moment…I'm feeling like it may be a lost cause. But damn, she got some good pussy…I'm not sure if I'm ready to give it up yet! Somehow…someway…I've gotta maneuver around this block she just threw in the road. Try to figure out a way to calm her down and get back on her good side….at *least* so ain't drama after this.

What Tianna thinks is true can only be followed up by a Sista Snapped incident. She's gonna be ready to resort to violence if she believes this shit.

I need to cover my bases…backtrack my steps. The *cheat gawds* usually look out for me in moments of distress like this – maybe there's a way outta this. Right now

2

though, it ain't looking good. She's all but convinced.

"HELLO?!?!?!" Tianna yelled at my silence.

"Yeah I'm still here," I answered quietly. "You wilding out right now."

Tianna started screaming excitedly, "Oh my *God* – no I'm *not,* nigga!!! I know yo damn voice by now!! I know what I heard – you not 'bout to make it out like I'm crazy! That was *you!!!*"

"How was it me when you on the phone with me *now?*" I deflected. "That don't even make sense!"

"Yeah, well that's what I'm trying to figure out," she paused as her voice drifted. "I think I know *hmmm*…yeah I think I got a good idea what's going on."

"What's going on Tee?" I asked out of real curiosity….to see how she's going to reply. What the hell is she thinking???

This shit is crazy man. This is the last time I let a nigga hook me up, I promise you. Fuck me!!! I mean really…I should have thought this whole thing out more thoroughly. How else could I expect this random **hooKup** *to play out? Truth of the matter is – I barely know this girl and she most definitely knows little about me. The way all of this started…it was bound to lead to this point. It was always only a matter of time.*

And why is she taking so long to answer my question?

3

I suddenly notice that she's now dead silent on the other end. "Hello?"

"Yep," at the same time Tianna speaks, I hear a phone ring in the back of the room behind me. Heart skipping a beat…I immediately freeze up.

SHE KNOWS.

Oh shit. My head starts to spin rapidly…and I bite my lip in desperation. My thoughts flash back to the night all of this started….

The Monday night after *KeLLy's Revenge…*

*　　　*　　　*　　　*　　　*

December 2003

I stood there in my towel for a few minutes after hanging up the phone with Cookie, gathering my thoughts.

This shit was really turning into a tangled web. I wasn't quite sure if I had lost the upper hand completely yet, but if so, I was at least regaining ground. I mean let's be honest…I never woulda found out *KeLLy* was cheating in the first place if *I* wasn't cheating. That's the whole beauty of the *Son's Curse* mixed with *The Art* – it's got a crazy way of bringing everything full circle.

Cookie was my mistress, my #2. It's kinda how the cards all fell in place during senior year at *CMSU*, so I

4

can't say it was planned out. The summer before senior year was wild, and while I did have a scheme to go out with a bang...before the fall semester I hadn't even *met* KeLLy *or* Cookie. And neither of them was on my roster.

Remember, KeLLy was a sophomore transfer from *TSU* in the Fall of '01 and had a boyfriend. Cookie was a freshman and first-year student from St. Louis. I was technically single and non-committed at the time – meaning I didn't have a girl as my main. You know the rules by now. So naturally, I was having my cake and eating it too.

Also remember, even when you're *'technically single'*, *The Art of Cheating* is still alive and well. In fact, *that's* where many of you *average* joes get y'all feet wet with being sneaky...when you don't answer to anybody. That's when you will lie to a muhfucka right in their face if they question you about where you've been or who you've been with. And since you don't owe anybody an explanation, you tend to subconsciously find yourself lying to who you're involved with. You keep your stable intact by not letting them know they're *actually* part of a stable. Oh sure, you'll let it be known that you see other people...but you don't tell all the details or facts behind what you actually *doing* with others. They don't need to know all'at cuz it's a competition for a position at that point. And just like any other candidate selection process goes...the individual candidates never truly know what's being done or said in the others' interviews. It's on *them* to be the best candidate *they* can be if they wanna be chose...

I was in no shape or form looking for a committed

relationship as a college senior. In fact, I was on a mission to fuck as many chicks as I could before I graduated. And like I said, the summer before senior year was *wild*. I must've banged 15 new chicks that summer alone – a record for me, maybe even a record for my peers if I remember it correctly. My high school crew was made up of a bunch of hound ass niggas. Every summer since high school graduation, we all participated in the 'race' – voluntarily or not, the *fuck-count stat* was kept between us. And like the last two summers before…in 2001 it came down to the same top 3 – myself, *Tre*, and *Lonnie*.

Lonnie and *Tre* were sideways hating on my 15 newbies and alleging that I was only getting more action because I was a *Kappa* now. There could have been *slight* truth to that – I mean it's no secret that the *Nupes* had a fan club that I took pure advantage of. Everybody is famous at some point, right?

But hell…these niggaz also knew I was getting pussy *before* pledging. The summer of '98, I beat out Tre, Steve, *and* Blayze with the fuck-count and *only* came 2nd to *Lonnie*. So, in 2001, it shouldn't have come as such a surprise to *any of the homies* that I would get the crown again. I wuttin' new to this. And both Lonnie and Tre had *cars* too…so they had the advantage on me for *years*. Nobody wanted to talk about *that* shit. But whatever. It was *no way* I could lose once I switched my roster to chicks who had cars only.

Going into my senior year in 2001, there was only one chick in the Burg I was fucking with. We won't say her *name* – but she was an *AKA* and she had a *Cadillac*

6

Escalade truck. Things were kinda taking a turn for the worse with her, so I knew once fall semester started...I needed to recruit early.

And that I did...

Cookie had a small frame, fat ass booty, and a car with low mileage. Three weeks into the fall semester of 2001, I was banging that three times a week. She was just what I needed as a senior – a young freak from the suburbs with hormones raging outta control. *And* she let me eat off her meal plan in the cafeteria on demand. Perfect situationship. By midterms, Cookie was the main chick on my roster.

All of this was *before* KeLLy...before I even *noticed* KeLLy on campus. Once Kells was in the picture, Cookie had some competition. KeLLy was a year older *and* had her own car. But the kicker was that Kells was from my hometown KC – which meant I could potentially see her more on breaks.

So naturally...there's always been tension between KeLLy and Cookie. Cookie hated the fact that I ended up in a relationship with Kells after I graduated and left campus for a while. But still...she never stopped fucking wit a nigga.

Cookie stayed around after she found out about KeLLy and she's been around ever since. She was here front and center to see me and KeLLy fall out this past weekend.

7

She's not gonna let this shit go.

And I'm not even sure what I'ma do with KeLLy now after all this shit. All I know is I'm on my way for some makeup sex tonight. I'm horny as *fuck*…and ready to release some frustration. Cookie is getting on my fuckin' nerves right now, pressing me about ending shit with KeLLy. And I don't know if I believe KeLLy fucked this other nigga or not. Tonight is all about one last nut for me. I just need some space from *all* of this shit.

I started to get dressed, throwing on some jogging pants and a hoodie. I realize that if I *do* move out of KeLLy's and back to KC…not only would I be giving up my in-house – I'm also leaving my #2 bitch behind in the Burg. And I ain't bout to get on the highway every single time I need some pussy…*right?*

Fuck.

That means I gotta fucking *start over*. I can't be sitting around with no pussy to pull up on, especially after a breakup. That's just unacceptable. And I ain't lived back in KC for a *minute* now. I been back in the Burg with KeLLy playing house far too long. Either way, I'ma need to reach out to my old resources.

I'm gonna need somebody to *hook me up*…

*　　*　　*　　*　　*

8

2

January 2004

Tianna was the first new chick I fucked with post-*KeLLy's Revenge*, and we got together via a classic *hooKup*. We started off chatting via *BlackPlanet* before quickly exchanging numbers and setting up a time to meet offline.

Tianna was younger than me, but about the same age as Kells. She was taking classes at *Penn Valley Community College* and working as a home health-aid parttime. The first time we talked on the phone, her country accent stood out. I found out she was from a small town in southeast MO, and had only been living in KC the past three years since her mom relocated. She had a proper tone and innocent vibe to her…but I could tell she was a freak. Most small-town chicks are…it's **SCIENCE**.

The night we finally met, we were on the phone before I headed to her *Grandview* apartment.

"Ok, for real…you better not be no psycho!" she warned casually. "Or a stalker or some shit!"

"Shut up, girl," I chuckled. "Ain't nobody 'finna stalk you! I'm too hot out here for all'at."

"Oh, whateva boy – you bet' not be *busted,* Rodney! All this shit you talking!"

"What if I am, though? What – *you gon' not let me in???"* I challenged her.

"Uhm…*yeah!"* Tianna reassured me. "Yo ugl'ass will be right outside my door! Think I'm playing if ya want to!"

"Naw I ain't worried 'bout it," I shrugged. "I'm more worried about you. You the one with the blurry picture n'shit!!!"

"No, come on – don't start! I told you my mama's scanner is raggedy!" she pleaded. "Whateva! I am *not* ugly boy – oh my *God!"*

"Well, we 'bout to see. I'm 'bout to be on my way after I stop at the store."

"I told you I don't really drink for real," Tee reminded me.

"Yeah, but I do, though. And I'm off tomorrow."

"And? What that mean?"

"You not gon' drink with me?" I pressured her. "You ain't gotta go in 'til noon!"

"Soooo, *aaaaaand???"* she smacked her lips. "No. I mean, I don't know. I might drink a little bit. I can't be drinking that stuff straight, though."

12

"Me either," I related. "Gin and juice. I got you."

"How far are you?" Tee wanted to know how long I'd be.

"I'll be there in about 20," I guesstimated. "I'ma call you when I'm outside."

I was on my way blinded...going off the word of somebody else that this chick was cute and not some wildebeest of a bitch. But like I said, I wuttin' in the Burg with Kells and Cookie anymore and I needed some new local pussy. It was worth a shot.

Tianna stayed alone and was fresh out of her own situationship, so she could use a new friend herself. She was more of a homebody than I was expecting and preferred that I meet her at her spot to hang out. She claimed that she had to stay close to home because she was on call with her job...but I wuttin' sure if I was buying that just yet. In my mind...this bitch just wanted to stay in on the possibility that we end up fucking.

We had been talking back and forth on the phone for about a week and a half now, and she had eluded to her mind always being in the gutter on the job more than once. But whenever I tried to keep talking about sex...she would stop me, telling me she can't be working herself up since she ain't getting none these days. That's what she missed most about the last nigga she was talking to...he used to fuck the dog shit outta her, and now that they done got into it – she's in a drought.

My plan was to seize the opportunity in this. She may not be down to fuck the first night, but a true *Master* in *The Art* has to be prepared for these type of circumstances, nonetheless.

I stopped at a liquor store about five minutes from her apartment complex off of *Longview Rd* and grabbed a fifth of *Seagram's Gin* with a bottle of *Sunny Delight Original*. They were having a post-New Year's Day sale on alcohol, so it was a win. Since I kept condoms in the glove compartment of *Annie Mae*, once I got the drinks, I was all set.

I said a prayer to the *cheat gawds*, hoping the bitch was fuckable at least. I had only seen two pictures of her so far. One from her *BlackPlanet* profile picture, which was small as hell, but I could tell she was caramel-complexed and not fat. Her face was turned to the side, and halfway covered with her bangs. The picture she emailed to my cell phone was a scanned image of a photo…a full body shot, but still blurry. She was obviously horrible at doing computer shit. But I could at least tell that she had some pretty big tits from that picture…at least a D cup…which looked huge on her smaller frame. Tianna looked to be in between thick-KeLLy and petite-Cookie from the pictures, but this was all taking place during a time where meeting somebody without seeing them in person *first* was risqué. If this chick turned out to be a bust…I was gonna be pissed to the max.

As I pulled up in the parking lot and stopped in front of her building, I suddenly realized that if all went well and I *did* fuck Tianna tonight…she would be the 1st chick on my fuck-count list for *2004*. Since being with KeLLy the past year and a half, I had slowed down some

– only smashing less than 5 new chicks last year. I wuttin' even in the annual race with Lonnie and Tre last year, but this was a new year and a nigga was fresh out a relationship again. It was time to get back in the swing of things…at all costs.

I pulled my phone out and dialed my nigga *Tre's* line.

"What up," he answered after the first ring.

"Aye nigga, I'm 'bout to try to fuck this little bitch! I just pulled up to her spot."

"Aww, yeah ok, nigga…we gon see!" Tre didn't sound like he had faith. "You been out the game for a lil min, Ro! I don't know…you might need some help finding the hole!"

"Naw whatever, nigga…you know better!" I felt disrespected. "I got this, cuzz!"

"Whatever blood…I bet you don't fuck her tonight then, nigga!" Tre talked his shit.

"Nigga, bet some money!" I snapped back with confidence. "I'm back, boa! We can bet I win the race this year, too, nigga!"

"What race Ro?!?!" Tre was one of few people who still called me by my high-school nickname. "Don't put ya foot in ya mouth, dawg – you ain't fuckin more bitches than me! I know *that* ain't what you 'bout to say '*bet*' on!"

15

"Nigga, how come I ain't?" I raised my voice in jest. "This bout to be number one for the year already and it's only the second week of January!"

"Ro – holla at cha boy," he stopped me. "I already fucked three new chicks this year, bro!"

"Maaaan…get the fuck outta here! You lying, nigga!"

"On the block bro – I did that. You still playing catchup, blood."

"Fuck you, nigga!" I shook my head. "I'm on yo heels, cuzz! Mark my words."

"Give it up, dawg!" my homie advised. "You been out the game, bro."

"Nigga, I took like one year off, fool," I blurted with dismissal.

"And this one shouldn't even *count* for real, nigga!!!" Tre kept teasing.

"I don't know why not!"

"Cuz you had to get *hooked up* with her, nigga!" he reminded me.

"And?!?! What that mean??" I was almost offended at the notion. "It's still pussy, nigga! Pussy is pussy and dis some pussy I ain't had yet! This counts!"

16

"Aye, I'm just saying," he laughed.

"Naw, nigga, you tryna be funny!!! Fuck you, nigga!" I cursed as another call came through. "I'ma hit you back. This her calling, bro."

"So, is it a bet?!?!" Tre wanted to confirm.

"Nigga, it's a bet," I poked my chest out. "But she count, bro."

"Aight, hit me back. Don't force yaself on her either, nigga!"

"Man, shut the fuck up, nigga. I'm hanging up."

Tre was still rambling when I clicked over and answered Tianna's call, but he was forever talking shit. I needed to get inside and see what this night had to offer. And Tianna was obviously just as anxious...as she was looking through her blinds at me in the car.

"Yeah, I'm here. I'm outside," I told her.

"I know," she acknowledged. "What are you waiting on? You scared?"

"Girl, shut up! Here I come. Which apartment again?"

"1-G," she said softly. "I'm 'bout to come to the front door, it's right when you walk in the building from this side."

"Ok. Here I come."

Her voice sounded sexy as shit! Maybe it was the adrenaline rushing through me at the thought of new pussy, but man this bitch sounded even sexier now that I was in front of her crib. I grabbed the liquor bag and locked my car up, hurrying towards the building. My dick was rock hard in my jeans…throbbing with anticipation…

*   *   *   *   *

3

She opened the door and all I saw first was legs. Long, oiled up legs busting out of her tiny ass shorts – shaking and shivering from the cold breeze.

"Hurry up…it's cold!!" she urged me.

She scurries on the other side of the door, holding it open for me…and I notice the lights are off inside, with only the glare from her tv lighting the bedroom towards the back. Once I stepped inside, she shut the door quickly, turning the deadbolt and hooking the chain all in one motion. I stood still until she turned around and faced me, her chest poking out. Her tits were *huge*. She had on a gray spaghetti strap little crop top with a scoop neck…and her breasts looked like they were going to rip it apart. I couldn't help but stare at her erect nipples pointing right at me.

"Dang, you ain't 'eva seen titties before?" she bit her lip. "I told you they big."

"I mean, damn," I felt the drool in my mouth building up. "You happy to see me?"

She covered her chest and stepped towards me, smiling hard. She was only a half inch shorter than me…and at eye level. "Oh, *whateva* nigga – it's cold!!!"

"Cum'ere…lemme look at you," I smirked.

"Dang, can I get a hug first?" Tianna frowned.

"No doubt," I turned to the side. "Lemme put this bag down."

I stepped into the kitchen, which was just a few feet from the front door and living room. I sat the bag on the counter before noticing the living room was completely empty. She noticed me making note of that and spoke up promptly, "You can put it in the freezer. And don't be talking shit, I told you I just moved in."

"I ain't even said shit," I grinned from ear-to-ear.

"Yeah, but you was 'bout to…smart-ass! You can take ya coat off…here, I'll hang it up."

She helped me get out of my coat and wrapped her arms around me before I could get it off completely – squeezing me tightly. Her tits were soft against my chest…and her body was warm as hell. She smelled like baby lotion and her fresh microbraids dug into the side of my face as she pulled me even closer…rubbing her right leg into mine.

22

"Damn, so you *are* happy to see me, huh?" I returned her lustful embrace.

"You smell good," she whispered, inhaling deeply. "What is that?"

"Hmmm...thank you, baby. It's *Nautica*," I replied in my bedroom voice.

"The plain one?" Tianna wondered.

"Naw, Blue."

"Oh ok. It smells good as hell. Damn," she held me for a couple more seconds before stepping back.

"You not gon let me come in and sit down?" I looked around in the darkness. "I mean, wherever we sitting."

Tianna laughed, "Yeah come on...we going to my room. My couches won't be here 'til the end of the month."

She takes my coat and hangs it in the closet next to the living room before grabbing my hand and walking towards the back room. The light from her tv is bright down the hallway...and I can see her a little better as she strolls in front of me – at least her back side anyway. She's kind of stout. She's got big, strong, and long legs, but her ass was just average and nothing like the apple bottoms I

23

was used to with KeLLy or Cookie. But them *legs?* Man oh man. Tianna's got track star legs...but I can't see her running no track with that rack. Ain't no way...her titties too big. She'd topple forward on her face for sure if she ran too fast. Then again, I *do* remember her telling me she ran track in high school...but gotdamn! I mean, I can almost see her round and plump tits from behind! The side boob action is epic in her crop top...and I'm feeling the blood below flow freely in my pants.

Tianna walks past her tv to the other side of the room where her dresser sits. The queen size bed in the middle of the floor has ruffled covers and sheets thrown all over. It's clear that Tianna is just as bad about making her bed as I am. That's when I'm suddenly reminded that I don't even have a bed of my own anymore and staying with my aunt is gonna get old fast. This chick barely has furniture n'shit in her crib...but at least she's got her own spot – more than I can say for myself at the moment after all this drama with KeLLy. I really need to take my mind off this shit...and not think about my reality for a little bit.

"You can make yaself comfortable...I'm just bout to watch *Chappelle Show.*"

"Hold on," I paused at the doorway. "Lemme make my drink."

"Ok."

I turn around and head back towards the kitchen as she climbs in the bed. My mind is racing. It's been a minute since I had some new pussy and the idea of it has taken over me. I can definitely feel a vibe between us...she ain't shy at all about me being at her spot after dark. But I still need to get a good look at her...it's dark as hell around this muhfucka. I mean...we've all fucked a ugly chick before. But my return to the sea shouldn't be me swimming with mediocre fish...not with my history.

And then, like I said before...with *hookups*, it's usually hit or miss. Although I technically have met other chicks off *BlackPlanet* before...this is the first time in a *long* time. And my nigga Tre was right – I been out the game for a minute. This could go either all the way good or all the way bad. I done got used to just fucking KeLLy or Cookie over the last year in the Burg. I mean, I've had an occasional one-night stand here and there – like that *Hangover* shit last summer – but nothing on the regular. And I ain't fucked Cookie since before she helped me catch KeLLy cheating...and ain't fucked Kells since the makeup sex afterwards. I started to worry about the three-week drought I was in and the fact that I ain't jacked off all day.

If it did go down with Tianna tonight...I might cum quick as hell. Good thing I had gin and some *Sunny D*.

*　　　*　　　*　　　*　　　*

25

Ok pause. So since I'm telling all my secrets here…I may as well spill the beans on the **Sunny D** *thing.*

Summer of '98

The year after high school graduation, my guy **Lonnie** *discovered that there was something in Sunny D that gave you staying power in bed. I know it sounds crazy…same thing I said the night this nigga called me about the shit. But believe it or not, this shit really works.*

Lonnie found out on accident, one night after we all left **Hot Summer Nights***. He dropped me off at this chick I was fucking named April spot, as usual, and he had action waiting with one of his jump-offs. The morning after, he called me with this crazy story about how he went to buy condoms and some juice after we separated…and he ended up getting a bottle of* **Sunny Delight***. He wuttin' really thirsty, so he mostly sipped on it on the way to the spot and by the time he got there – he had over half a bottle left. His girl was still in the shower, so he said he watched* **Sports Center** *and kept sipping like it was alcohol instead of juice. Lonnie rarely drank liquor anyway so when he's telling me that he's sipping it like some alcohol, I know that mean he sipping this shit slow as fuckin' molasses.*

Well anyway, Lonnie ends up falling asleep waiting on the bitch to get out the shower and she wakes him up like 45 minutes later. They get to doing dey thing…and Lonnie says that after he let

26

one off…he got right back up within minutes — and goes **another** *round. Now remember, we both* **19** *at the time and only a year outta high school so the idea of going round after round back-to-back is some superman shit. I swore the nigga was lying and must've been on some drugs or some shit…but Lonnie don't even smoke. He goes on to tell me the next round lasts longer than ever before and he had to actually* **fake** *a nut to stop fucking. The nigga said he literally fucked 'til he was falling asleep in it.*

"Nigga, but how you know it was the **Sunny Delight**, *dawg?"*

"Bro — that was the only thing it coulda been!" he broke it down. "I ain't drink shit else that night. I'm telling you, it's something in that juice."

I still wuttin' buying it, "But nigga, you always drink that shit! That makes no sense, brodie."

"I know, but that's what I'm saying — you gotta sip that shit, like it's a drink. I ain't never just sipped it like that. I'm telling you that's what it was," Lonnie campaigned.

"Man but how you **know** *tho?" I thought the whole idea was silly. "Cuzz, I'm not 'bout to believe dat shit, dawg. You tripping!"*

"Bro, I'ma do it again tonight. I betchu it works…I know I ain't crazy. You can believe it or not if you want to. Don't say I ain't hook you up, though!"

"Maaaan. Ok. Aight bro, we gon try that shit. We gon see," I finally gave in and called Lonnie's bluff. "I'll probably need a ride over April's tonight, too. Let's just grab some then."

"Aight, I'm for real dude. Don't tell nobody this shit if it work," he advised carefully. "Shit, I already know it's gon work but you know what I'm saying?"

I laughed, "Yeah…if the shit real, we got some secret weapon type shit, my nigga! Aight, that's wassup. We gon see, cuzz."

And that we did. The two of us went on an experiment spree after that to see what the fuck was going on and I'll be gotdamned – the shit actually worked. It has to be original flavor, and you gotta sip on the shit slow…about an hour or so before you get ya freak on for best results. And best-case scenario – the shit is like some liquid **Viagra**…no down time. **Sunny D** became my secret supplement weapon and Lonnie's **hooKup** proved to be an instant classic…

*   *   *   *   *

January 2004

So now I'm back in Tianna's room with two cups of gin and a bottle of *Sunny D*. I made her drink much more watered down than my cup…with more juice than gin. Mine is *Big Boy Status*, low on ice and heavy on the gas. I'm

28

sipping the *Sunny D* right out the bottle instead of mixing with my liquor. It works better that way.

Tianna is on top of the bed and I'm sitting at the foot on the floor, looking up at the TV in front of me. The season premiere of the *Dave Chapelle* show is about to come on and we've both gotten comfortable. She's still in her crop top, but now the shorts have come off and she's under the cover in her panties. I've pulled the jeans off to lounge in my gym shorts and wife-beater.

"Why you sitting on the floor?" she wondered. "I'm not gon bite you."

"I'm cool right here, I'm not trying to tempt you," I replied smoothly. "We just chilling."

"Oh, whateva boy! You always talking stuff!" Tee snapped. "See…that shit remind me of my *ex*."

"I thought y'all wasn't really together," I raised my eyebrow, recalling our previous conversations about former flings.

"Well, you know what I mean…that's what I be saying. You sound like him with all'at shit talking."

"Man, I ain't that nigga!" I felt offended. "I told you quit comparing me to him! Fuck that nigga."

"I'm not comparing you," she insisted softly. "I'm just saying you got that slick ass mouth like him…that shit irks me!"

29

"So now I irk you?"

"No…I ain't saying that. I mean, it's not the *exact* same – you more smooth and laid back – but y'all both be talking that slick shit!" she explained. "'*Oh, I'm not trying to tempt you, baby…that's not what I'm here for.*' All'at slick ass shit!!! *You know what I mean, boy.*"

"I'm *not* trying to tempt you, though," I insisted matter-of-factly. "I'm just being me."

"How you know I don't want you to tempt me, though?" she posed a good question.

"Do you?" I snapped back without hesitation. She better quit playing with me.

"I ain't say all'at."

"So, what you saying, then???"

"Nothing boy! Be quiet. You bout to make me miss *Chappelle*," she tried to switch gears.

I played along, keeping my cool, "Man you need to get on that *Crank Yankers!!* I'm telling you! You sleep."

By the first commercial break, Tianna's moved down towards the foot of the bed. She's still laying up top…but now her face is to the right of me and she's rubbing my head through my du-rag. She's got small hands, but her grip is firm. The way she's applying just the right amount of pressure at her fingertips is giving me major fuckin' goosebumps. I ain't had no head rub in weeks. She can tell I'm feeling it, too. I mean, I'm not being subtle about it – my body language wouldn't let me. My head was leaning back and I was looking up at the ceiling in total bliss.

"You ok?" she asked to be sure.

"Yeah. That shit feel good as fuck."

"Are you tense or something, boy?" she swiftly grabbed my collarbone and squeezed gently. This catches me off guard and my left leg jerked…. knocking my cup of gin over on top of me, spilling my drink all over my shorts and her carpet.

"Gotdammit!" I yelled with instant frustration.

"See…look at you!" Tianna hopped up and I moved to the side, lifting my shorts off my leg.

"It's yo fault!" I frowned, turning my nose up at the strong liquor smell. "You did it!"

"Hold on, lemme get a towel."

She runs out to the hallway, and I presume she's going to the linen closet. By the time she comes back in with a green towel, I'm standing up wiping my shorts down with my hand.

Tianna stops me, handing me the towel, "Just take

31

'em off. I can wash 'em real quick."

"Then what I'ma wear while you wash 'em?" this sounded like a setup. "Stop playing…"

"Boy, shut up! You scared to be in ya underwear around me??? I'm in *mine*…"

Indeed she was. But if I took my shorts off, it wuttin' no way to hide my stiffy and I ain't want her to be able to read my mind. I mean, I'm sure by now that we both got the same thing on our minds, but I still wanted to play it cool. I ain't like how she was comparing me to her last guy. She needed to get over that nigga. And my goal was to show her something different…*to hit her with a different angle that she couldn't see coming*. It's kind of been a silent vow of mine since we first started rapping on the phone.

From our first conversations, Tianna was saying I reminded her of him…how some of our comeback phrases were the same, how we were the same type of asshole. This nigga hurt her feelings pretty bad, apparently. And she was irked at anything that made her think of him. In *fact*, our first few talks didn't go over too well…as she was almost ready to stop talking to me altogether because I reminded her of this nigga so much. The shit was weird. She even asked me if I knew his ass, showed me his *BlackPlanet* page and everything. After that, I was like 'enough is enough.' I had to ask…*what the fuck did this nigga do to you, girl?*

She told me that she was talking to her ex for almost

32

a year and things were pretty serious. She had only been with one other guy since moving to KC and this *Tyrone* cat was the first nigga she ever had feelings for. She said they spent damn near everyday together and he would even bring her lunch on the job at her client's crib.

She was really comfortable with Tyrone cuz she felt like she could talk to him about anything, and she opened up to him about how hard it was after her father died. He had lost his dad at a young age so he could relate to her trauma. Tianna found herself madly in love with this man and thought they were a perfect match.

Especially sexually. Tianna had a high sex drive and Tyrone was the first nigga who could wear her out in the bedroom. She liked to go round after round sometimes; other times she wanted a quickie. Tyrone knew how to give her just the right type of dick at the right time of day.

She says they had a good thing up until right after she invited him over for Thanksgiving dinner with her family. She claimed they were supposed to go see the Christmas lights on the *Plaza* afterwards...but then he had to leave early all of a sudden. When she questioned him about it, they fell out. After that night, she noticed a change. Tyrone came to see her less and the sex went away. He suddenly wouldn't talk to her for real anymore, and she couldn't get through to him for some reason. By Christmas, he'd stopped calling her back *completely* and she was devastated at the fact he could just walk away from what they had just like that.

Tianna was obviously hurt and needed healing. And

now that I was in the picture – every little thing I did…reminded her of the ex. I clearly had my work cut out with this *hooKup*.

"Yeah, you sholl right," I looked down at her lace panties, deciding it was only fair that she wuttin' sitting around in her underwear alone. "Ok."

I pulled my shorts down to my ankles…and now I'm in my boxers, semi-hard underneath. Tianna takes my shorts without looking down and walks out the room. I flick the light switch on and start to wipe myself off. There's gin dripping down my leg and on my foot. Looking down, I notice Tianna's empty cup on the floor.

This bitch took that drink to the muhfuckin head! This is craaaazzzzy.

I can hear her walking down the hall back towards the bedroom. She's already started the washing machine…sounds like it's in the bathroom.

She turns the corner…and it dawns on me again that I still never got a really good look at this chick's face…

*   *   *   *   *

4

Tianna stepped back into the now fully lit room smiling from ear to ear. She looked *Blasian* in the face, with a mole on the left side above her lip. Her teeth were straight and not gapped...lips full and shining with pink gloss. She stood there in the doorway staring me down with slanted eyes, giggling.

"What's so funny?" I asked curiously.

She was cheesing hard, "Anybody eva told you you look like *Ray J?*"

"No," I lied.

"Well, you do, kinda," she told me, before lowering her voice. "But you cuter, though."

"Whatever," I waved her off.

She stepped in front of me, frowning, "Awww, poor baby. I'm sorry, cum'ere."

Grabbing the towel out of my right hand, she started wiping my boxers down...even though I had dried 'em off already, for the most part. My dick had gone limp and was

37

hanging still…but now that she was rubbing my leg, he was starting to swell up again. She was bent over slightly, head at my chest as she leaned in to rub me down. I could see her ass crack at the top of her dark blue panties and below the tattoo on her lower back.

"Don't be looking at my tramp-stamp, either," she mumbled, reading my mind.

"Yo what?"

"You heard me! My tramp-stamp," she repeated as she stood up and stared me in the eye.

"Why you call it that?" I lowered my voice.

She leaned in closer, and now her lips were inches from touching mine, "That's what it's called. That's what it is."

"Hmmm," I bit my lip. "I see."

She was standing so close I could smell the liquor on her breath. And she was breathing hard. Not loud…but hard. My dick jumped…hitting her inner thigh. "So you happy to see me now, Rod?" she took a half step back…looking down.

I grabbed her, pulling her back in closer to me. I wanted her to feel it up against her body, "What you think??"

"Boy, you betta quit playing with me," she warned

seductively, stepping away again and biting her lip.

"Ain't nobody playing," I raised my eyebrow. Her eyes were locked on my boxers and I was making him jump every other second now.

"*He* is," she pointed at my **wooD**. "Mmm hmmm. Tell him he better stop."

"He better stop what?"

"Stop playin', Rodney," she tried to shake it off. "Make me another drank."

That was a good idea, actually. We both could use another.

"Ok," I agreed. "Am I still gon' get my massage?"

"I got you, boo. Hold on, I'll be right back."

Minutes later the lights are back out. I'm laying in the bed on my stomach, shirt off. Tianna is on top of me – her ass on mine, legs spread across my lower back with her knees bent. She's giving me a back rub that's outta this fuckin' world. She starts dripping warm baby oil all over my back and wiping me down firmly...running her nails across my skin.

Damn...did she go microwave that shit?

39

Either way, she's got skills.

She goes from open palm presses to a smooth circular knuckle grind…climbing up my back and following up with a steady shoulder grip. All in rhythm…all in the perfect flow at the perfect pace. She's even better with her hands than KeLLy…and Kells was no joke on the massage tip. It's one of the things I loved most about my sex life with KeLLy…she could calm me down and put me in a trance just touching me, working kinks out of my body before she took advantage of me. Very few girls got a chance to be in control with me…and KeLLy knew how to make me give a little up. It all started with her hands….and right now, Tianna was breaking me down with her touch like I had never been broken down before.

I couldn't help but moan as she leaned in closer…whispering in my right ear, "You good?" All I could smell was gin…but all I could feel was lust.

"Yea…that shit feel good as a muhfucka."

"Yeah, you need to relax," she urged. "Let me do what I do."

"I ain't stopping you," I pointed out, matching her bedroom voice.

"But will you?"

"I mean – what all you tryna do?" I started wondering.

"I'm giving you yo rubdown you wanted," she tried to sound innocent.

"Ok, then."

"Ok then," she repeated mockingly. "Take yo boxers off."

"For what??" I asked. I wasn't used to taking demands like that.

"So I can rub you down," she whispered in my ear. "Everywhere."

"Maaan...you *playin*..."

"Naw, nigga...*you* playing," she cut me off, pressing down on my lower back. "You playing with that drink, too."

"Shut up," I shot back. "I can't drink it with you on top of me like this."

"Well, come on and catch up, Rod," she challenged me. "You babysitting."

Damn this bitch ain't playing around with this gin. She rolled over to the side and grabbed my cup off the dresser, shoving it in my face. I barely had it out her hand before she took her own her cup to the face, swallowing big gulps like it was water. Her tits were bouncing with every slight move and she noticed me staring down at 'em.

41

Biting her lip…she put her cup back on the dresser and lifted up her shirt…pulling it over her head and tossing it to the floor. "You happy now? I know you wanted to see 'em. Yo ass can't stop mugging."

She's absolutely right. I can't stop staring. The glare from the TV was shining behind me…but the moonlight beaming through her two windows on either side of her bed provided just the right amount of light in the room. Just the right amount of rays highlighting her chest. Her fucking tits were perfect. I mean perfectly perky and round…and her areolas looked drawn on. Her nipples were hard as fuck. But they look like they don't never be soft – immaculately complimenting the magnificent work of art. They're so much bigger than what I'm used to – much bigger than *KeLLy's* C-cups. And they make *Cookie's* A-Cups almost irrelevant.

"Are these muhfuckaz *real???*" I was in awe.

"Touch 'em. See for yourself."

She ain't gotta tell me more than once. I scooted closer and started grabbing and squeezing like a baby exploring. My jaws dropped. They were real indeed…naturally soft and heavy. I couldn't help but wonder how they sat up so gotdamn perfectly.

She was closely watching my every touch, staring down at my hands as I rubbed her slowly. I pinched her nipples briefly as I grazed past. She loved having her breasts played with…that much was evident. My dick was hard as fuck now and poking out the bottom of my

42

boxers. Tianna peeped and grabbed it by the head…pulling at it. Then she lets it go just as quickly.

"You gon' take ya boxers off so I can finish ya rubdown???"

I licked my top lip and kept squeezing her titties, "Yeah. I got you."

"You gotta lay on ya back, though," she smiled before scooting away, pulling her chest out of my reach.

My dick jumped again. She's not making this easy.

"Come on," she urged again.

As I sat up on my knees and started pulling my underwear down, she took another big gulp out of her cup. Then she suddenly gets up out the bed and walks towards the TV stand, reaching for something on it. I ain't pay it much attention…as I followed suit and finished my drink, chasing it with two sips out the *Sunny D* bottle. I laid back on the bed, resting my head against the headboard.

Now I'm fully naked – dick laying on my stomach…hard as stone. Tianna turned around and stood at the foot of the bed. She took a long stretch…reaching her hands in the air. Her bust was unreal in the shadows…and I could see that her stomach wuttin' the least bit flabby.

Damn. This bitch is sexy as fuck…

43

"You ready???" she interrupted my thoughts.

"For what???"

"For me to finish," she ran her tongue across her teeth and walked around the bed to my left, approaching me slowly. She stumbled as she got closer, giggling.

"What are you trying to do, girl?" I knew she was up to no good. I could just feel it.

"Come onnn…you said you not gon' stop meeee," she cried out.

"Stop you from doing *what,* Tee?"

She didn't answer. Instead, she climbed on the bed and rubbed her hand on my left thigh. I noticed she was holding something in her other hand, so I sat up a little more to peep the scenario.

Tianna leaned in again for a whisper, "Lemme tie you up."

Aww HELL NO!!!!

I was suddenly attentive and alert…my radar on level 5. I hated being tied up. I had only let one chick, *Destiny,* do it years ago in college. Destiny liked to blindfold and handcuff me so she could have her way without me touching or stopping her. Complete fucking torture. I ain't never been able to deal with the loss of control since. I mean sure – *Destiny* used to fuck my brains

44

out and drain me every time – but the idea of not having my hands free just *fucked* with me.

Tianna knew how I felt about this, we had that talk a *week* or so before this link up. We was talking about what we liked and didn't like…and she was telling me how much tying a man up turned her on. *Tyrone* never let her put him in restraints and now she was really craving that shit. I told her I could understand why he wouldn't and I was the same damn way.

So, then we started talking about other things we were craving…and she starts talking about how she ain't had no head in almost *two years*. I thought that shit was insane. How was the sex with Tyrone so damn good *without head?* She told me that he just never wanted to do it, he claimed he never ate pussy in his life. She loved the nigga so much that she just went without oral. His dick game was good enough without it for a while. But then she started craving it later in their relationship and now that she was in a drought…she said she's been dreaming about some good ass head. So, I told her I was craving the same thing…even though I'd be surprised if I ever got some head better than *Cookie's* head.

She wanted to know what made *Cookie's head* so good. Not because she was curious, but because Tianna rated her own mouth better than most and believed she was likely just as good. I told her Cookie just genuinely enjoyed sucking dick and she especially liked to swallow. At the end of this exchange, Tianna tells me that if we ever end up having sex, she'll give me what I'm craving if I give her what she's craving – and we made a little deal.

45

But now…she's talking that *restraint* shit and I was just talking *head*. I can't do the restraints…fuck that shit, yo.

"Naaaah…I told you I don't like being tied up," I protested firmly.

"Come on…I ain't gon' blindfold you," she promised. "Come on…"

She straddled me, sitting on my dick. Her pussy was warm and moist through her panties.

Shit.

"Lemme get what I'm craving," she continued. "I'ma play fair like you said."

"Maaaan," I felt cornered.

"Say yes," she's leaning in closer now, and we're face to face again. She sticks her long tongue out…touching the bottom of her chin.

Shit!! Her tongue is long as fuck.

"See, you *playing*…"

"For *reeeeal*…I'm not," she insisted. "I'm drunk as fuck, too. I told you I get hella freaky when I drink! Why you get me drunk?"

"I didn't get you drunk!!" I argued, hoping the subject changed. "Don't be blaming that on me."

She reached behind her, grabbing the base of my shaft, and squeezed hard, "Yes you *did!!* Oh my *GOD!!* You feel how wet I am???"

"No."

She hopped up suddenly and was standing up in the bed. Looking down at me, she pulled her panties off swiftly. Her pussy was hairless...and the lips poked out in the front. She rubbed it in front of me with her right hand, then bent down close to me again, putting her wet fingers in my face, "See? Look what you did."

"Look what *you* did," I grabbed my dick in agony.

"Lemme take care of it."

"How??"

"What you been craving..."

"*Fuuuuuuck...*"

"For real," she pressured me. "Lemme suck it."

"Go ahead," I consented without a second thought.

"But you gotta let me tie you up, though," she

47

reminded me, crushing my eager hopes again.

See dat's dat bullshit!

"So you not gon' suck it if I don't let you *tie* me up???"

"I'ma suck it regardless."

"Yeah?" my eyes widened.

"Yeah. But…if you let me tie you up," she paused mischievously. "I'ma swallow it like *Cookie.*"

"*Swallow* it….?" I gulped.

"You heard me…swallow it," she repeated herself with sass. "*All of it.* Every drop."

"Come onnnn," I whined. "Stop playing…"

She dropped down and had my dick halfway in her mouth before I could blink again, drenching and drooling all over my shit. Spit started running down my shaft, onto my balls, and down on the sheets….and she started stroking my dick up and down with her right hand. She was moaning with every stroke. I threw my head back and licked my lips – and gave a big thrust upwards. As soon as I did, she lifted her head up and looked me back in the eye…her left eyebrow raised above her kinky eyes, "Lemme tie you up Rodney…"

*　　　*　　　*　　　*　　　*

5

This bitch is not playing around....

My shaft was shining in the moonlight…sloppy wet from Tianna's juicy mouth…and she was kissing my thighs, waiting on me to agree to the restraints. I knew I would regret it later, but it's hard to make a conscious decision with a hard dick, rubbing against her huge tits.

I took a deep breath and slowly gave in…whispering loudly, "*Ok. Ok…*"

"*O…k? For real???*" she popped her head up with excitement.

"Yea, man. Hurry up, before I change my mind."

She doesn't hesitate. Before I could even get situated, she was standing over me again. With both my hands in hers, she pulled my wrists together and wrapped a small piece of rope around them.

Where the fuck did she pull that rope from? This bitch couldn't wait for me to say yes!

She's moving so fast all of a sudden – especially to

51

be so drunk. The room was still dark, but the light from the TV and moonlight gave me just enough to see the evil grin on her face as she swiftly crawled down toward the end of the bed to tie my ankles together, too. Now my hands were behind my head, wrists tied together as tight as my ankles.

Tianna started slowly climbing back up towards me. She ran her fingernails up my leg before digging into my skin. It hurt…but at the same time, it didn't hurt.

Once her face reached my **wooD**…she stopped with a long stream of drool hanging from her lips. She looked up at me with mischief in her eyes. I couldn't believe I was letting her do this shit. In my mind, I came over here on some *'cool'* shit…but as I looked down at Tianna now, I admitted to myself that this was kind of part of the plan. Give her control of where she wanna take things….and end up with the upper hand in the end. My hands being tied wuttin' in the strategy, though. I can only hope she keeps it reasonable.

Fuck.

I've got a bad habit of comparing bitches to porn stars…but I'm used to it, so y'all should get used to it, too. In this moment, Tianna looked like a splitting image of the black porn legend *India*…looking me dead in the eye while she bobbed up and down my sloppy wet manhood, stroking it with her right hand. I started squirming like crazy…biting my lip with split emotions – one half disdain, the other appreciation. I needed some porno shit like this…if only for one night.

52

Still, I couldn't get over the fact that I was tied up. Tianna was holding me down by my waist...chasing me all over the bed...conquering me with her mouth the same way I had learned to dominate with mine so many times before. I was laying halfway on my right side now – humping her throat.

Well, wait. I was *trying* to hump her throat...but she was meeting my thrusts with more anticipation than I had thrust...and swallowing me whole with ease. Balls deep...she began forcing her head even further...trying to fit my whole fucking pelvis in her mouth.

Then I felt her tongue. I'm still in her throat....and her tongue is circling my balls underneath...

What...the...FUCK!!!!!!!!

I can't take it anymore...and I start to let loose...grunting and moaning, biting my lip and cursing. I could feel the thick cum shooting out, Tianna was taking every spurt in gulps. She pulled up briefly, to jack it off and watch it shoot...and I throbbed in her hand as she stuck her tongue out...trying to catch the next shot. Her tongue was long as all outdoors...my mouth was wide open watching her work. She cut her eyes at me and shoved me back in her mouth...poking her jaws with my head and sucking hard.

I'm squirming again.

Tianna kept sucking and started rubbing my balls with both hands...squeezing them slightly, making me

53

scoot away. She's staying true to her promise…swallowing me dry. But once I was all out of nut…she *kept* sucking…slurping and drooling, keeping me rock hard.

"Damn, girl," I groaned helplessly.

"What, nigga?"

Tianna was full of cockiness. I wanted to grab the back of her head and slam it down on my dick as I squeezed the back of her neck. It's killing me to not be able to reach down at her and I started pulling my left hand towards the sky…trying to break free. The knot felt slightly looser than before…but it was still tied tight as fuck.

Tianna glances up and sees me struggling. Abruptly, she stopped bobbing her head and stared me in the eyes with rage.

Then it happened.

She starts to run her *teeth* up my shaft as she pulls up off my dick…eyes cut low.

"*Fuck!!!*" I yelled out. "Bitch, what the fuck is wro…"

"Quit trying to get loose, then," she demanded sternly.

"Man, don't be biting my dick n'shit girl!! You out yo muhfuckin'…"

Before I could finish, her left hand was in a claw and digging her nails into my abdomen. I started kicking my legs apart...trying to break my feet free. Tianna just smiled at me, scooting away to the side of the bed as I desperately tried to get outta my restraints.

"What you call me, *nigga*?"

"Aye, untie me!"

"Naw, what you call me, nigga? Say that shit again..."

She gets up in my face. I tried to bite her nose but she pulled away...then quickly leaned back in to lick my cheek...getting my face wet with her spit.

"*Bitch, I'ma...*"

"Yeah...that's what you said," she cut me off. "That's what I *thought* you said."

She reaches for the rope around my hands, and we're in the bed struggling now...me flipping around and trying to knock her body away. It doesn't work. Her track star legs were wrapped around me within seconds and she had me pinned down, staring at my bloodshot eyes.

"Stop moving," she commanded.

I bit my lip angrily, "*Fuck you!*"

"You 'bout to. Stop moving. *Be still.*"

55

I eased up momentarily…and she tightened the knot on my wrists even tighter.

"Man nah, you play too *much!!* Let me loose – *for real.*"

Tianna looks down, "Yo dick still hard, though."

It is? Man.

"No, it ain't," I tried to deny her discovery, but my shit was hard as steel. "*So???* Untie me!!!"

She leaned in and started kissing my neck, licking and running her tongue across my shoulder blades with lustful passion and horny rage. Then, wet kisses down the middle of my chest…licking across to each of my nipples. She stops at my left nipple and starts sucking and kissing on it…reaching down with her right hand to grab my dick. It was still wet with her mouth juices…and she started squeezing it in the middle of my shaft. Hard.

She's sucking my nipple hard as fuck. The longer she sucked, the stronger the suction got. The shit felt surprisingly amazing.

She started squeezing my dick harder and moving her lips across my chest back and forth to each nipple.

The sucking gets even *harder.* My dick is *pulsating* in her hand, just as hard. And then…outta nowhere…she

56

fuckin' BITES. MY. NIPPLE.

As hard as she could.

"Aaaargh!!!!!" I screamed. *You bitch!!!*

"There you go again!" she responded devilishly.

"Bitch, there *you* go again!!!!" I felt her hand gripping even harder before she leaned in and bit the fuck outta my other nipple. "Bitch, quit *biting* me!!!"

Tianna lifted up again, her tongue out and mouth open wide with a line of drool hanging. I started pulling my head back and squirming as she came up towards my face.

This bitch bet not get drool on my face!!!

She must've heard my thoughts. Because then she suddenly moved down and ran her tongue down my dick with spit balls forming out the side of her mouth. Her lips wrapped around it from the side, she started going up and down with scary intensity.

And then I felt her *teeth*. AGAIN.

But this time she was just grazing slowly. No pressure…just super light friction.

Dammit!!!

She keeps moving her head up and down…slipping

and sliding with her teeth against my sloppy wet shaft. I start shaking. Shivering. It feels way too tingly. I'm getting goosebumps…

Then she takes me in her mouth again, slurping and sucking slowly. It was real animalistic. She held herself up on one arm and grinded her massive tits against my leg as she went to work, digging her nails in my ankles. My eyes are rolling. I'm starting to feel dizzy.

*This muthafucka really loves this sick shit!!! Lowkey…I think I do **too** at this point. But I still wanna break loose. I need to grab this bitch, regain control. Ok. Focus, Rod.*

I'm watching her suck me slowly. She's really into it now, not looking up. All I can think about is how I wanna choke this bitch out when I get loose…how I want to bite her until she screams for mercy.

I start twisting my wrists frantically, but without moving my lower body. The knot is definitely loosening, because now I can pull the rope down my left wrist a little.

I just need to keep twisting and turning and I'ma get outta dis shit before she know what's happeni…

"You undoing that knot???"

"No," I answered immediately, my body stiffening up.

Tianna looked up at me with her hands on my balls…holding my dick in front of her face, "You *lying*, nigga!!!"

Without warning, she hopped up off the bed towards the dresser, looking at herself in the mirror before walking around to me on the other side. She reached for my wrists and I closed my eyes tightly…shaking my head.

Fuck!!

"It's ok…I got some shit for yo ass," she threatened. "I'll be back."

And with that, she stormed away into the shadows…stomping down the hallway towards the front of the apartment.

The TV suddenly went blank.

How the fuck…???

The room became engulfed in still darkness.

Man, what happened to the moonlight? Did she close the blinds?

Two seconds went by. Then two more as I strained to listen closely. But the only thing I could hear now was my heavy breathing and my heart thumping in my chest. Everything else went dead silent.

Tianna had disappeared without a trace.

*   *   *   *   *

6

"Aye what the fuck, man??!?! Where yo ass at?!?!?!" I yelled at the silence.

This bitch got me all the way fucked up!

It felt like a whole minute had passed. I could barely see shit in the room now, and I was lying real still, trying my best to hear what was going on. When I closed my eyes, my hearing seemed to get stronger. I started to make out the faint sound of the heat blowing from the furnace…which I ain't even notice was on until now.

THIS IS DAT BULLSHIT!!!

If this bitch come back in here with 2 goons and a power drill…that's just what the fuck I get! What the fuck was I thinking letting this bitch tie me up?!?! I barely fuckin' know dis bitch! One of these days, Rod…you gotta stop thinking with yo dick!!!

My stomach starts turning and flipping. The gin is starting to settle n'shit. I hope I ain't gotta throw up.

For a quick half-second, I heard Tianna walking around out in the hallway again. But then for real, I wuttin' sure if it was somebody in the next apartment or upstairs above us. Sound is so confusing in the dark.

Man, fuck this. I need to get out of these gotdamn knots, bro.

If *Lonnie* and *Tre* could see me now, I'd never hear
the end of it! *Especially* Tre – that ignant ass nigga gon talk
all types of shit 'til the end of time about this one. Tre was
Mr. Go Hard on a Bitch...he wouldn't let a bitch tie him up
for a million plus 1. Hell, I couldn't imagine Tre being into
half the shit I did with hoes *in general*...our styles were
opposite in nature anyway. But *this* shit – I mean this shit
was *way* outta bounds...even for myself.

Then, at the same time, I couldn't wait to get outta
this bullshit so I could tell them niggaz what happened.
Anything else would be uncivilized – this whole fiasco is
classic, nonetheless. And never in a million years would I
keep this story to myself...the crew lived for these
moments. This was what *The Art* was all about – the
adventure. Whether I was the butt of the joke or not
didn't matter...this was all for the archives...all in the
name of the game.

I most definitely hear footsteps now...and I can see
a faint hint of light coming from the hallway. As she gets
closer, I see the light flickering, and she slowly walks in
carrying two small candles, "Rooooodnnnneeeeeeyyyyy."

This hoe is ill.

"Aight, quit playing, Tianna!!! Let me go."

She walks over to the dresser...sitting the bright red

candles down. I can see a lot better now. I notice the rope around my ankles is purple.

What the fuck is this bitch doing with purple rope?

"See, you just had to start fucking up," she shook her head. "Now I gotta punish you, Daddy...."

"Maaaaan, see dis dat bullshit I'm talking about! And you wonder why niggaz won't let you tie 'em up!!! Let me out, for real!!! Quit playing with me!!!"

She took a step toward the bed....and then hopped in the air and on top of me...legs locked around me.

"*Or what?!?!?* What you gon do? You can't do shit – you tied up, nigga!"

I let out a long sigh, "Bitch, I swear to God..."

"See, there you go with the names again," she pointed out. "You just never learn."

She put her hand around my neck and leaned in...hard nipples rubbing my chest. My dick jumps.

"Get off me!" I yelled.

She was clawing at my chest. Not hard...but not soft either. The look in her eyes was filled with lustful evil...she had fire in her vision. Before I could react, she took my nipples in both hands...twisting and pinching. HARD.

65

"*Aaaaaaaarrrrgh!!!!!*"

Once I let out another yell…she shifted up and bit the shit outta my shoulder.

HAAAAAAAAARD…

She started pinching and biting…biting and pinching…all over my upper body and chest area. Randomly picking spots – twisting and turning with me as I tried to fight her off.

BITE…PINCH.

…PINCH. PINCH…then another BITE.

"Bitch, when I get out this muhfucka I'ma beat yo *ass!!!*"

"No, you ain't!!! Well, get out then!" she challenged me. "Come on! Fuck me up, Rodney! *How you getting out???* Huh???"

She's poking me with her nails…grabbing my cheeks.

I can't believe dis bitch!

"You want me to let you out???" she asked softly.

"Yup."

"You gon act right???"

"Yup…I am," I told her what she wanted to hear.

"You *lying,* nigga!" she snapped back to the femdom terrorist voice. "*Niggaz are liars!!!* Stop lying to me!!!"

She hopped up off the bed again and now she was back at the dresser. My chest and stomach burned from the bruises and scratches. The insides of my wrists were sore…it felt like skin was broken. Still, I was trying with everything I had to get loose. Pulling at the rope…trying desperately to get my one of my wrists to slip through.

I see her coming back towards the bed out the corner of my eye. I don't care. I've gotta get free…

This time, though, she doesn't stop me. Instead, she just stood there for a few seconds….one hand rubbing and squeezing her tits, the other rubbing her pussy as she squirmed.

"You crazy, bitch," I snarled.

"Call me a bitch agai…" she let out a moan as her voice drifted off.

My left wrist was making leeway. I looked away from her and up towards my hands…which I couldn't see since they was behind my head. Before I could blink…I felt her mouth on me again…licking and sucking my balls. Drenching me.

67

That made me stop moving as my body collapsed and went limp on the mattress. I felt helpless. The room started spinning. For a split second, I almost thought I heard voices in my head.

"Stay focused, Rod. We getting outta this shit."

What the fuck, man? This bitch really got me tripping.

I closed my eyes and relaxed momentarily as she took my half limp dick in her mouth again…sucking it hard. She starts to get nasty with it again…wetting it up with a thick coat of spit forming around it. This bitch is sucking my soul out. I swear…if it wuttin' for all the weird shit – she'd give Cookie a real run for **Head Queen**. Cookie just owned the dick when she gave head. This bitch Tianna *kidnapped* and *raped* the muhfucka.

I'm starting to build up again…and then suddenly Tianna stops sucking and heads for the dresser. I just stared at the ceiling…waiting for her to get on with it. She gets back on the bed lightly…slowly.

And then it happened.

ONE DROP.

TWO.

THREE. FOUR DROPS…

This bitch started pouring *candle wax* on my thighs – and then my naked stomach and chest.

68

I immediately flinched...then I laid still again. It burns...and then...it...doesn't. Just as quick as it hit my skin...it cooled down and hardened.

She's squatting over me...reaching under her pussy to play with my dick....and the other hand was pouring wax on my stomach and chest. After a few more drops...she slid the candle on the dresser and started kissing my neck again...whispering, "Hmmmm...you know you sexy as fuck, right?"

"Mmmm hmmm."

"But, I can't let you loose."

"Why not???"

"Cuz I don't trust niggas," she said with bitterness.

"You can trust me..." my voice sounded groggy for some reason. I almost didn't recognize it.

"*STOP LYING!!!*" Tianna screamed viciously.

"I'm not lying."

"*All* y'all niggas lie! You can't help it."

"Let me out this rope, girl," I demanded.

"Oh, now I'm '*girl*'???" she was full of sarcasm. "What happened to all'at '*bitch*' shit?"

"Maaan...fuck you!"

"Aww yeah???" she lifted her head up and bit my left cheek. "You gon' fuck me???"

"Yep, *I'ma fuck the shit outta you*," My reply was automatic. I could feel my stomach rumbling.

"You *promise??*" she asked with a hint of excitement. "I'll let you go if you promise. If you promise you gon fuck the shit outta me and make it hurt."

"*Let me loose.* That's what I'm 'bout to do," I let out a growl.

Why am I growling?

"Nah, I don't think you can gimme what I want," Tianna decided. "You ain't ready."

I started biting at her face in rage and she quickly moved away. Frustrated, I stick my tongue out...trying to jab her face with it. Big mistake. Tianna grabs it with her teeth like a wild tiger.

Fuck.

I laid still.

VERY STILL.

Tianna keeps her grip on my tongue, staring me in the eyes. Suddenly, I can't hear anything anymore. It's like

70

I've gone deaf.

I'm breathing slowly. Mostly at her pace…but more so out of nervous fear. My heart is racing. The hairs all over my body are standing up. I feel a tingling surge shooting up my back…it damn near stings. It seems like time is moving in slow motion. I've never felt like this before.

My main side bitch…

I started thinking about how I got here. Flashbacks of Cookie on the other end of the phone – telling me I was a fool to trust KeLLy. My toes started twitching.

KeLLy…

Images of my ex laid up with Marcel flood my head. Suddenly I'm even less sure about whether I believe she ain't fuck that nigga. I'm getting upset all over again – but it feels like a different type of angry. It's damn near vengeful. I start to feel light-headed, as if I'm 'bout to pass out. A stream of drool runs down the side of my chin…and I can't tell if it's from my mouth or Tianna's.

Tianna…

My eyes start blinking again with Tianna on top of me. She's reaching behind my head…grabbing at the rope.

Is she untying me??? She is. She's letting me loose…

I can feel her pussy leaking on my stomach. My dick

jumps twice.

I still wanna fuck this bitch. I wanna choke her. Bite her face. She knows dat shit, too. She got me right where the fuck she want me.

Tianna finally lets my tongue go and sat up straight. Looking me in the eye, she whispered, "Fuck me, Rodney."

I pulled my hands apart, ripping away at the loose rope. Aggressively, I sat up straight, pushing Tianna to my right side. She flopped on the bed like a rag doll and let out a yelp. In a split second I was reaching for my ankles.

"Come on, nigga…what you waiting on???" she whined impatiently as I started tugging at my lower restraints.

Tianna then started scooting up towards the headboard and opened her legs, feet planted on the mattress. Her pussy was soaking wet. I could hear her stirring around the juices with her fingers. Once my feet got loose, I flipped over on my knees and turned to face her.

My hands then moved upward and found their way to her feet. Soon as I made contact…Tianna moaned and shuddered. I started squeezing her toes.

Her feet are soft as fuck. Damn, I can't believe her skin feels like this. Then again, I ain't never really touched nobody's toes. Mostly KeLLy's.

72

I get lost in the moment again for a second, talking to myself in my head before kneeling down to Tianna's left foot and lifting it up towards my mouth. I've never sucked toes. I've never even wanted to. But without hesitation I took all of her toes in my mouth with thirst-filled passion.

Tianna goes crazy and starts twisting and turning, still rubbing her pussy. For some reason, this pisses me off. She's enjoying this shit too much.

In response, I stuck my teeth in her foot. *HARD.* She sinks in the bed...moaning and groaning.

I then threw her foot to the side and leaned in, climbing on top of her to lick her stomach. My tongue traces her torso up to her cleavage. Taking one tit in each hand, I started squeezing and grabbing. Pinching her nipples. Biting and grabbing her small neck.

"Fuuuuuuck, nigga!!!" she winced. "That shit *hurt!!!*"

"Shut up, *bitch!*" I snapped.

Tianna gasps, "O...ok Daddy. Ok."

I started sucking her nipples aggressively. They were rock hard against my tongue...but soft when I bit down. She pulled me closer and now my left knee was grinding against her pussy.

It's running like water.

I grabbed her neck and squeezed hard, making her gasp for air, *"You little nasty bitch! I should choke the shit outta you!"*

She started coughing, reaching for my neck. I slapped her hand away and released my grip before she blacked out on me.

Now I'm back down at her stomach. I lift her up by her ass cheeks and dig my nails in. My rage is starting to come out. She feels it too…and she's rubbing her huge melons with force and anticipation.

Her pussy is staring at me. Throbbing. Leaking…

I dive in tongue first…hands still cuffing her ass. Then I run my tongue up her lips and to her clit…and start sucking like a madman.

She starts grinding against my face…moaning loudly, "Oh my GOD…that feels so goo…….FUCK……shit, NIGGA!"

I pulled my hands off her ass and her cheeks hit the bed while I reached around to grab her ankles. I forced her legs up towards her head, putting my weight up against her as I kept sucking her pussy. She's completely submitting and not fighting me at all…her big strong legs now up under my forearms.

And then it happened.

74

I took her clit in between my teeth....

....and I *bit down*...

...............**HARD**.

*   *   *   *   *

7

…but not too hard. I mean…it *is* a *clitoris*. If I bit her for real, I could bite the muthafucka off.

No…I bite her clit *just enough*…so she knows I can play unfair too.

She jumps away in shock…screaming and reaching for her crotch, "*You punk ass nigga!!!*"

"Bitch, what you call me???" I hopped on top of her, all *hundred and sixty-five pounds*…and I was in her face in a half second, biting her cheek and pinning her down.

"Nothing, I'm sorry," She sinks into the bed. "I didn't mean it."

"Bitch, yes you did! You meant all'at shit! Got bite marks n'shit on me…burning me with *wax* and shit! What the fuck is wrong with you?!?!?"

I flip her over and start smacking her ass…hard slap after hard slap. She's wincing and bracing herself…and I'm slapping harder and harder. She keeps yelling and cursing with each slap. With one last smack, I cuff her cheek and dig my nails in…clawing slowly and deeply as she arches her back in response. Then I take my right thumb and shove it in her pussy, lifting her up by her pelvis with my other fingers while pressing down hard inside of her.

She's losing her mind.

I lean in…biting her cheeks…licking up to her back, biting down as I thumb-fuck her. My dick is jumping as I'm bent over on top of her. She feels it bouncing around and reaches under her crotch to grab it. Her hands are soft…and *wet*.

Did this bitch lick her hand?

Nasty bitch. I love that shit.

She's jacking me off…and I'm fucking her with my thumb, rough and stiff. Her juices are splashing, "Yesss! Fuck…oh shit…fuck…*yesss*!"

"You like that shit?!?!" I grunted. "Huh? *You hear me, bitch?* You like that shit?!?"

"Yessss," she panted, gasping in between breaths. "I hear…hear…you…I…I…."

"You hear what I said…*BITCH???*"

"YES! I do!!!"

"*BITCH.*"

"YES…?"

I've never talked to a chick like this in bed. I don't know what's come over me. At this point, it feels like I'm in a trance. This shit is turning me into an animal.

"Did you hear what I said…*bitch???*" I repeated with more aggression.

"I hear you…yes…*FUCK*…*me*…I hear you!!!!"

Lonnie and Tre will never believe this shit. But *Stevie* will. *Stevie* graduated a year ahead of us and he's been telling us for years that chicks love to be dominated and called out their name when you fuckin' 'em. I mean, I would never imagine it took all this shit to go there…but right now, Tianna has awakened a beast in me. I'm still mad…mad as *fuck* that she tortured me and had me in pain and agony…all at the same time that she was sucking the skin off my meat. I wanna fuck her…but I also wanna hurt her. I wanna make her just as mad as I'm feeling right now. It's a hard, drunk, and horny rage…filled with liberation and passion.

I've always felt this inner spirit deep down inside. But until tonight, it felt like nothing more than dark, sinister, kinky thoughts. Until tonight, my innermost desires felt trapped in a cage.

But tonight, I wanna let this beast loose. And so, I do just that.

I pulled my thumb out of her and hopped off the

bed...fumbling around on the floor looking for my jeans. I've gotta get a condom on quick.

"Daddy," Tianna whispers.

"Don't move, bitch," I commanded. "Stay right there. Just like that."

She arched her back...ass in the air, rubbing on her pussy with three fingers, "Come on, Daddy...come fuck me. You said you need some pussy. Come on. You see this pussy? You see...this...come on...."

"Shut up, bitch. I'm coming."

I stood at the foot of the bed and tugged her by the ankles, motioning her to scoot towards me. She complied without making a sound...moving back on her knees until she was close enough for me to grab her by the waist. She reached under to grab my dick.

"Bitch, move yo hand!" I barked at her. *"Be fucking still..."*

I'm just now getting to know this beast inside. He's aggressive and mannish. I like him. This slut Tianna will love him.

"Spread them cheeks."

Tianna pulls her ass cheeks apart and I see her asshole is shaved bare. Damn. I can't help but drool in it. She moans loudly, "Oh my *God*...are you gonna..."

"Shut up, bitch!" I cut her off.

"Noooo! FUCK me, baby…I need that dick. Gimme that dick!!!" she whined impatiently.

I smacked her ass cheeks again before shoving my dick in her wet and tight hole forcefully. She moved forward on the bed, trying to run from it.

"Cum'ere," I snatched her back towards my thrusts. I need her to take this dick like a big girl.

She doesn't miss a beat. She starts throwing her ass back, meeting my long strokes in sync, her cheeks slapping against my thighs, sounding off.

"I…*said…DONT……MOVE!!!!!*" I reached forward, taking her microbraids in my hand. Jerking her neck, I started pulling her head back towards me as I put my back into my thrusting.

She's screaming and cursing at me, "Fuuuuck…you! You…you…nigga…fuck you, nigga! Damn! Oh – my – *God!* Fuck *me*…right there…*SHIT!* Shit, nigga! Damn! Let…let my…*hair…go!!!!*"

She tried twisting her head and her body away from me, but I had a firm grip on her braids, my elbow resting in her back. I'm humping fast and out of control…like a dog in heat.

Tianna kept panting, "Come on! Come…*on!* I feel…*feeeel* it!! Come……*oh* my…I'm bout ta…I'm bout…to…"

"You 'bout to what, bitch???" I bit my lip, snarling.

"Come on. I'm 'bout to fucking *cum*. I'm 'bout to…don't stop…."

"Don't tell me what to do, *bitch!!!*" Just then…I pulled out of her pussy and walked towards the dresser.

Tee crashes down on the bed in frustration before rolling over on her back and slapping her pussy lips, "Nooooo!!! Why…whyyyyy, Daddy…????"

I paid her no mind. By now I had a candle in my hand…leaning over her, still standing next to the bed. She sees my intentions and grabs her right breast…holding it out for me.

No hesitation.

ONE DROP. TWO DROPS.

I turned the red candle all the way upside down…pouring wax all over her stomach and titties.

She screams and yells in pleasure.

I can't believe this shit…

I threw the candle to the floor and the flame went out, making the room dark again.

Pushing her to her left, I climbed in the bed and mounted her, forcing her to hold her legs up in the air. Guiding my dick in slowly...I started biting her lip. Her pussy clenched around my **wooD**...causing my body weight to crash on top of her. She then started biting the side of my face near my ear...and I nudged her head away with mine, biting her shoulder and licking as I held my teeth in place. My hands were around her neck.

I kept beating her pussy in, "You nasty bitch!"

She kept taking it, clawing and scratching my back, "You like it tho...*don't*...you? *Don't you* like it???"

"Bitch! You...ever...pinch....me...*cum'ere!!* Don't ever fucking...*think* – you tying...me up......agai...."

"*Oh* damn, nigga!!! O......K...OH...*KAY* nigga...I won't! I won...hmmmm *fuuuck*...ok, *okaaay*!!!!"

"*SHUT THE FUCK UP!*" I shoved my fingers in her mouth...muffling her sounds. She started licking and drooling on 'em, getting them wet. Her mouth was so fucking warm. I yanked my hand away from her lips...wrapping my arm around her leg, cuffing her ass again. Then I started rubbing her hairless asshole...fingers wet with spit...her ass wet with sweat and pussy juice.

Tianna grabbed my ass cheeks...pushing me deeper, squeezing and clawing as I kept thrusting. My index finger was in her ass...just the top part...and she sunk her teeth on my shoulder, "I'm...I'm...cumming! I'm cumming! Oh my *God*...Rodney I'm fucking...cum...cummi...

hmmmmmmmmmmmmmmmm......"

Her pussy muscles were squeezing my dick.

TIGHT.

.................*TIGHTER...*

GRIP......RELEASE. *GRIP...RELEASE...*

...and I started cumming again. *HAAAAAARD.*

I pulled my finger out her ass and regained my balance...long stroking and lifting up in the air before I slammed back down into her. She's squirming and now has gone silent, mouth wide open and staring at the ceiling as I pounded it. I'm dripping sweat on her as I hit it.

She looks up at me, locks eyes, and starts to wipe sweat off my face, "Come on baby...come on. Give it to me...hmmmm!! I wanna taste it..."

I pulled out soon as she said that...reaching down to pull the condom off. She sits up promptly and reaches down to help...leaning forward as I leaned back and put my dick in her face. Then she started sucking and stroking...finishing me off.

I fell to my side and she kept sucking until I slapped her in the face...pushing her away. She moaned in satisfaction...still playing with her pussy while I laid still for a few minutes.

The next thing I know...I'm knocked.

OUT.

*   *   *   *   *

The next morning, I woke up early – around 7:30. Tianna was sleep next to me...head on my chest, slobber everywhere. I pushed her off me with no consideration...and her face hit the pillow hard.

"Fuck you, nigga," she mumbled.

"Fuck *you*."

I got up and limped to the bathroom in the hallway. I felt sore. Wore out.

I need to get the fuck up outta here...asap.

So after I took a piss, I looked around for a towel...so I could take a quick hoe bath.

"Aye where yo towels at???" I yelled at the walls.

"Whaaaat?"

I opened the door a little so she could hear me, "Where yo towels at, man???"

85

"Look out in the closet…."

"What clos – oh ok, never mind. I got it."

The water is running now and I'm soaping myself up when I heard a loud knock outside the bathroom.

I immediately turned the faucet off. Listening….

Am I tripping?

"You good???" I asked, frowning up.

She doesn't answer so I turned the water back on and started scrubbing again.

I wonder if she got any big towels. I might as well take a shower over here before I go back home to my aunt's.

Then I heard it again.

3 LOUD KNOCKS.

BOOM! BOOM! BOOM!

It's coming from the front door.

I hear Tianna curse and hop up off the bed,

86

knocking shit over. She runs to the bathroom
door…whispering from the other side, "Oh my *God!!!*
Don't say *mothing!* Be quiet…ok???"

*   *   *   *   *

8

So now I'm sitting in the bathroom ass-naked. On the toilet. Quiet as a church mouse.

Whoever was at the front door was beating nonstop now.

This dat BULLSHIT.

I could hear Tianna running around frantically, getting dressed so she could open the front door. She was cursing and stomping around...obviously mad that she was woke up like this. I started looking down at the scratches on my arm and stomach.

Damn, she got me pretty good. What the fuck is going on, though? The last thing I need is some drama on the way out the door after last night. This already been one crazy ass **HooKup**.

There were voices coming from her living room, but I couldn't make 'em out. Sounded like another chick. Maybe a little boy...but it was hard to tell. I heard footsteps in the hall and then Tianna yelling again.

WHAT. THE. FUCK...

The front door slammed. I heard bumping against the wall in the living room…or it coulda been the kitchen. Then, footsteps.

The bathroom door flew open with Tianna on the other side. She was in a bath robe and motioning for me to come out, "Hurry up before my mama bring my lil brother back. Fuck! I forgot I'm 'spose to be watching him this mornin'. Come on…"

"I'm coming, gotdammit! Shit. Calm the fuck down."

"You calm down," she pinched my arm as I walked past.

I immediately slapped her hand away, "Aye man, don't start that shit…"

"Damn," she frowned. "So grouchy."

I moved through her room quickly, getting all my shit together. The whole scene was trashed…looking like her spot been robbed. I tripped over the empty *Seagram's* bottle…shaking my head, "Damn…we got it in in dis muhfucka, huh?"

"Right. Got me drunk n'shit."

"Don't be blaming me…fuck that."

"Whatever," she snapped back. "You took advantage of me. Niggas ain't *shit.*"

I shook my head, "Girl, you crazy."

"I know. When am I gonna see you again, though??"

"Soon."

*   *   *   *   *

So later that night I'm rubbing *Neosporin* on my scars after soaking in Epsom salt for an hour...gathering my thoughts.

The first question a nigga asks himself after some new pussy is simple: *Would I fuck again?*

That one was a no brainer...at the same time that it was a mind-twister. I mean...the pussy was good. Tianna had this insatiable appetite and wetness that was out of this world.

But shit...I can't be doctoring myself up every time I get some ass...and that restraint shit gets old quick. I still wanna choke this bitch out for even taking it there with me. Something happened with me last night. I ain't never called a chick out her name so much...or been so damn rough. This bitch had me sucking toes n'shit. Damn.

I started to get horny just thinking about it.

What the fuck is this about? Have I discovered a new level of kink in myself?

My thoughts were suddenly interrupted by a phone call from *Cookie*. I answered on the first ring, instantly mad, "*What?*"

"Hello?"

"What, Cookie?"

"Hello???" she repeated in frustration. "Why you answer the phone like that?!?!"

"Why you been calling my line so much lately?" I was irritated.

"I mean, you not on *Yahoo* no more and you ain't down here," she started explaining. "Boy, I can call you!"

"What you want?"

"Oh, for *real?!?!?* I gotta want something???"

"I mean...you usually do."

"Ugh!! You get on my nerves!!!!" Cookie pouted. "When are you coming down here?"

"I'm not," I said dryly. "For what?"

"What do you mean for what?" she gasped. "I mean, don't play. You know you are *not* done messing with you-know-who."

92

"Girl, whatever…"

"Yeah! So, stop fronting and just let me know when you coming back – so I can see you."

"I'm not coming back no time soon," I tried to tell her.

"So, you just moved back to Kansas City? Just like that???" Cookie sounded shocked.

"I got a job up here now."

"And you just broke up with KeLLy???" she kept pressing.

"Let it go, Cookie," I sighed.

"No! I will not let it go!" she yelled. "Who you up there screwing?!?!"

"Bye, Cookie."

"*Rodney Lee Henderson, Junior*…don't you hang up the phone on me!" she screamed frantically. "Hello?! *HELLO!?!?!*"

"I'm still here."

"Ooooo, you get on my nerves! I *miss* you! Why won't you come back down here, for real?"

"Where is yo *man* at, dude??" I shook my head.

"He's at the community center playing ball," she answered calmly. "See, that's why you should be down here. I could be sucking your dick right now."

"Whatever…"

"Don't act like she give you head better than I do," she blurted out with arrogance.

"Who you talking about??"

"Whoever you been sticking yo dick in! I know you been up there sleeping around. That's why you not down here. You can't replace me though."

"Man I'm 'bout to go…"

"Nooo!!" she protested.

This time I do hang up.

Cookie was right. She was hard to replace. She was ranked the GOAT on my **fuck-count** as of then. She knew exactly what to do with the dick…knew exactly how to touch and kiss me. The shit was like porn every session…minus the Tianna-antics. Sex with KeLLy was almost as good…but she wasn't nasty with it like Cookie was. Cookie wasn't afraid to get slutty and degrading…she would get lost in the moment and not think about what she done 'til afterwards. KeLLy was much more reserved – much more hesitant to act unladylike, even in the bedroom. At any rate – distance-wise – neither KeLLy nor Cookie was close enough anymore, and I needed to figure

94

out if Tianna would stay on my new roster to be...

But before the night was over...I had to get my niggas Lonnie and Tre on the three-way.

These niggaz gotta hear all about how this shit went down....

*   *   *   *   *

The next time I talked to Tianna...we went into all the details about our epic night. Most of it was a blur to me, but I could remember the important parts.

First and foremost, I made it clear that the restraints wouldn't be happening again. Before I could start going off about it...she told me that she won't ever crave that again. She just needed to get it out her system one time with me...and she knows that after she got that off...I'ma always fuck her the way she needs to be fucked. She needed me to be rough and disrespectful...dominant and angry. But she says she can't help the biting, pinching and scratching. And she wants to be tied up. She wanted me to manhandle her...force her to do shit she objects to at first. She wanted me to push the envelope with her...and fight through her resistance.

The shit gets outta hand. We start fucking on the regular. I mean every Wednesday night like clockwork. But it gets to the point where I stop through her spot during some workdays…to get a nut off on a lunch break or some shit. She *loves* for me to make her suck my dick on demand…she loves submitting to me. I even start pulling up on her at her clients' crib while they slept in the other room or upstairs. Quickies in the bathroom, sneak fucks in the garage.

Over the next month and a half I added two more to my new roster…but they didn't compare to or get priority over Tianna when it came to the dick. Tianna got first priority every time. Even when KeLLy was in town a few times after that, I shook Kells to go fuck Tianna. I'd feel guilty…but not guilty enough. Not yet.

The shit gets even more crazy.

As it starts to warm up mid-March…Tianna started craving *anal sex*. She talked about how I play with her asshole every time we fuck…and how she's only had anal with one other guy years ago. She tells me Tyrone was too big and wuttin' into anal, anyway. She then gets on this long tangent about how different I am than Tyrone in bed and how much more freaky I get with her. She just wants to be able to let loose and do all the kinky shit she thinks of and she says I make it easy to express herself and explore that side of her. So, she makes me promise that next time I come see her – I'll go *backdoor*.

To put it in perspective, I'd only done anal with KeLLy – and only twice when we were *pissy* drunk. But at this point – somehow, for some reason – Tianna had unleashed my inner **beast**. She knew it…and I knew it.

*   *   *   *   *

So, we were supposed to hook up for anal the day after *Usher's 'Confessions'* album was released. I remember because Tianna was a big *Usher* fan and she couldn't wait to have the album in hand. She was jealous because I had the bootleg copy for almost a month before...and would cuss me out when I tried to get her a copy earlier.

She calls me about two hours before I was supposed to come over...in a sad mood.

"What's wrong *Tee Tee*??" I asked, sounding as concerned as I could.

"Maaan...I just got off the phone with my *ex*."

"Yo ex? The *Tyrone* nigga?"

"Yeah," she admitted.

"Ok. And?" I failed to see the issue. "What's wrong? What happened???"

"We got into it," she started explaining. "He get on my damn nerves, I swear."

"What y'all get into it for??? I mean, I thought y'all was done."

"We are. But...I mean...he's been calling me lately.

97

Acting like he misses me. Playing with my emotions."

"Right. Well, I knew y'all been talking again."

"How *you* know?" she wondered.

"I just knew. Don't worry about it," I said. "So, why y'all get into it though?"

"He just was tripping!! Asking me about the new nigga I'm fucking, talking about how I'm hurting his feelings and shit! But that nigga supposedly laid up living with some chick now I heard anyway!"

"Wait...you told him about me???"

"I mean yeah...he was acting like he *already* knew n'shit! And plus he was pissing me off talking shit so I just told him! Yes, I been getting dick and quite often!"

"Wow," I blinked my eyes in disbelief.

"Yeah, he didn't like that shit!" she told me. "Oh well. I do feel bad cuz he usually don't show emotion. But, oh well. He need to be hurt the way he did me."

"So, then what happened??"

"Nothing...he started going off and I hung up. Fuck him...uhm," she paused. "Hold on. This him calling. Hold on, baby."

She puts me on hold and clicks over. It's obvious this

guy wants to keep her head spinning around. I'm shaking my own head, yawning.

This bitch is so clueless.

Tianna was yelling as she clicked back over, "Oh my *God!!* I can't stand that nigga!"

"Hello???"

"Yeah. My bad, baby," she apologized. "But yeah...so that nigga tripping."

"What you mean???" I asked curiously.

"Talking about he gonna pull up and kick my door in if I have any niggaz at my spot. Boy, whatever! This nigga don't even know where I live! He think I still stay by my Mama."

"Man, I ain't bout to be coming over there if ya lil ex dude gonna be tripping," I told her.

"Fuck him! He not coming over here," she tried to convince me I had nothing to worry about. "He don't even know where I stay, baby."

"You don't know *what* that nigga know! *Who* he know or who he *fuck* with!" I yelled back. "Nah man...I ain't 'bout to come over there tonight."

"I know you not scared of dis nigga!!!"

99

"I don't know that nigga to be scared."

"You said y'all played ball at *State Line,*" she reminded me.

"I said I seen him up there playing before. I ain't say I *knew* dat nigga."

"Well, whatever!" Tianna smacked her lips. "You know this nigga I'm talking about and you know he just all talk. Always talking shit! Fuck him. He not coming over here. You better bring yo ass and quit playing. For real."

"Maaaan," I let out a long sigh.

"For real...he is not coming over here," she said again. "I need to see you. I need to nut. I need some dick."

My dick started twitching, "See, there you go...."

"Whaaat?" she whined. "And you supposed to give me what I'm craving. You supposed to hook me up."

"Tee Tee..."

She lowered her voice, "Come on...don't do me like that. You still coming over???"

"You know I am," I had to admit. "I'll call you when I'm on my way."

"Ok. Don't forget the lube either, nigga!"

"I'm not, bitch."

"Fuck you, nigga!" she snapped at me. "I *got* yo 'bitch'."

This shit is about to get crazy, bruh.

*   *   *   *   *

9

On the way to Tianna's later that night…I got another phone call.

Not from Cookie.

Not from Lonnie...or Tre…

But *KeLLy*.

Every time I seen KeLLy's name flash on my screen….my heart skipped a beat. Every time. Even up 'til that day…she still had that effect on me. I would never let her know this was the case…I was determined not to give her the upper hand back.

I was still hurt…still dealing with insecurities from her creep incident. I mean, for a cheater like myself, you would think I could just brush the shit off. But like I've said plenty of times before…you never think it can happen to you. It's a fucked-up way of thinking and moving – but it's the simply an absolute truth in *The Art of Cheating*. More than anything, though…I was starting to feel *guilty*.

KeLLy had really been on my heels since we took

some time apart and was trying her best to make things right with us. She was on a mission to prove herself to me...to prove that we could move on from what happened and be a happy couple again. As long as I kept her at a distance...I could go on with my belligerent ways and not think about it. But every time she popped back up or was visiting town, I froze up and got all soft. She still had my heart. She could convince me to spend time with her at any time if she wanted to. And again, I couldn't let her know just how much of a hold she still had on me – so I always had to gather myself before answering the phone. Put my game face on...*ya dig?*

"Hello," I cleared my throat.

"Hey babe..."

I hate when she calls me that.

"Hey Kells...what's going on?"

"Oh nothing...just got out the shower," she replied. Was thinking about you."

"Awww...that's sweet. Are you in the city?"

"I will be this weekend. Why...you wanna see me?"

"Uhm...I didn't say that," I shook my head.

"Mmm hmm. How long are you gonna play this game Rodney??" she pressured me.

"What game, KeLLy?" I acted clueless.

"This *'playing-hard'* mess. I mean...it's been three months. You know I love you. You *know* I'm not fucking with anybody. I only wanna be with you. You know this."

"Yeah. But you know I'm not ready, too. I told you I needed time. I'm not playing no game. I just...I need time, KeLLy."

"Ok ok. Ok. I get it. I'm not rushing you. I just need you to know I'm here...I'm not going anywhere," she explained herself. "I miss you. I know you need time...but...I just wanna see you, be around you again."

"I mean...I miss you too."

"You don't have to be scared to tell me that, Rodney. I know you miss me too."

"I just said I do," I started to get annoyed.

"I know. I'm just saying. I miss you, too. I know we're meant to be, I'm not gon stop believing that. Just don't give up on us yet, babe. Ok?" Kells kept playing on my emotions.

"I haven't given up yet."

"Yet?"

"You know what I mean, Kells," I sighed.

105

"Ok ok. I'll take that."

"Ok," I rubbed my eyelids.

"So, am I gonna see you???" she asked again.

"I don't know…"

KeLLy chuckled, "You must got you a new lil girlfriend up there or something now. Who keeping you away from me, Rodney???"

"Shut up, girl," I snapped back. "It ain't like that."

"Oh, so you gonna act like I don't know you now?" she teased. "I know how you do, Rodney."

"We not together right now Kells," I said in my defense.

"Ok…you right. I'm a let it go," she let out a deep breath. "Even if you are doing yo thing – I'm still not giving up, Rodney."

"Ok, KeLLy," I decided to let it go. "Listen…I gotta go. I'll just call you later. Or call me tomorrow when you get to the city."

"It'll be Friday," she confirmed, matter-of-factly.

"Ok, just call me then."

"Ok. I love you," she whispered. "You don't have to

106

say it back."

"I know I don't. But I will. I love you, too. Bye Kells."

As I pulled up at Tianna's spot...all I felt was guilt. Good thing I had some Gin and **sunny D**. It had become a regular routine that I bring gin and juice whenever I came to see Tianna. She was a sweet girl sober. But with some liquor in her...Tee turned into a certified porn star. By now, she was the go-to chick when I needed to let loose...which was becoming more and more often...now that I had gotten used to the 'war zone' we created every time we fucked.

My inner beast was finally out the cage now, with nothing to hold him back...and I had Tianna to thank for it. Before I fucked her...I was way more reserved in how I expressed myself sexually. The beast was a summation of all my rage and letdown...all of the built-up adrenaline that before had nowhere to go. Sexual frustration can sometimes feel like sharp teeth sinking into you, over and over again without warning. After being bitten one time too many...Tianna now had me on a mission to let the beast bite back.

She was submissive for the most part...but she loved pain...dishing and taking it. The last few times we got down, it got crazy...borderline violent. But it was natural for the both of us now...and no one ever called the police after all the punching and biting and scratching and slapping. The more aggressive she got...the more aggressive and dominant I became...and she knew this

107

would be the case. She knew from that first night that once she pissed me off enough...I would give her angry dick every time. I was starting to get concerned about the lasting effects now though...how would I ever cage the beast again? Most chicks couldn't handle my aggression before. Post-Tianna...a whole different type of creature had been created. And the beast needed to be fed constantly so I didn't have to think about my real world of emotions and incomplete situations.

So even though I knew that this bitch was loony and unstable...I kept going back. And now tonight...I was set to go *backdoor*.

Tianna left the door unlocked for me, as she usually did now. I walked in and went directly to the kitchen and made our drinks. When I walked to her room at the end of the hallway, she was already naked...rubbing her titties in the bed, "Took you long enough, nigga."

"Don't start, girl," I warned her.

"Shut up. Gimme my drink."

"Fucking alchy," I licked my lips, handing her the cup. "Here."

"And take ya clothes off," she lowered her eyes.

"Don't be bossing me around, girl. You don't run shit."

"How come I don't?" She sat up on the bed and

started grabbing at my shirt, lifting it up so she could rub my stomach. My dick started growing down below soon as she clawed at my abs.

"Damn, can I sit down and drink first?"

"Ok, but hurry up nigga," she said impatiently. "You know I'm horny when I get out the shower."

"Why you rushing me?" I wondered. "You expecting company???"

"You being funny, nigga???"

"I'm just saying. You got crazy ex's n'shit."

"I told you he don't know where I live," she reminded me. "You ain't got shit to worry about."

"Like I said," I bit my lip. "You don't know what he know."

"Whatever," she waved me off. "I don't know what that's supposed to mean but he ain't shutting down shit or running shit over here."

"I think you want him to know you fucking me," I accused.

"Maybe I do."

"See? You on that drama bullshit…"

109

"I'm really not. I mean…I'm not mean. I don't wanna hurt his feelings."

"You said he act like he ain't got feelings."

"Cuz he *don't!!*" Tianna yelled. "For real…y'all act *just* alike when it comes to that. I swear I thought y'all was twins or some shit when I first started talking to you."

"Oh, here you go with that shit," I rolled my eyes.

"Shut up nigga!" she grabbed my arm from behind and pinched it real good.

"Man, I'ma fuck you up, girl!"

"Hmmmm, I hope so," she grinned. "Damn, at least take yo pants off though, nigga. Don't act like you ain't never drank with me in yo underwear, nigga."

"You always talking shit."

"You love my shit talking, though."

"I love your *mouth*," I corrected her. "There's a difference."

A half hour later…Tianna was sitting on my face…and we were in a sixty-nine. Some females out there say that sixty-nine is overrated and they prefer not to cuz it's hard to concentrate when getting some good face. Tianna would disagree. Nothing can distract her from sucking good dick…she makes it hard for me to

110

concentrate with her skills.

So, she's slurping and sucking and making all types of noises while she grinds her pussy on my face...rubbing her clit on my chin. She bites my inner thigh...I bite down hard on her right ass cheek. We both moan and groan in pleasure and agony.

"Stick ya finger in my ass, baby," she whispered with lust.

"*Bitch*, I got this."

"Hmmmmm, fuck I love it when you call me a bitch like that," she melted as she started stroking my dick fast...which was soaking wet from her mouth.

I tried to hump upwards at her, and she put her weight down on my legs to hold me in place, "Be still, baby..."

"Fuck you," I snarled. "You be still."

"I *caaaaan't,*" she squirmed. "Hmmmm. Yeah...lick that shit, baby. Just like that. I'ma cum on yo face."

"I'ma cum on yours," I moaned.

"Noooo, don't cum yet...save it for my ass, baby," she urged me. "I wanna feel you cum in my ass."

111

Fuck. This girl is so damn nasty…

I pushed her off of me. She wuttin' expecting it so she fell face forward against the bed…cursing under her breath.

"You so nasty," I revealed my thoughts to her.

"You love this nasty bitch, though, nigga. You ready to fuck me???"

"Yeah, lemme get a condom," I tried to sit up.

"Nooo, baby," Tianna stopped me. "You don't need a condom for my ass. You bring the lube?"

"Yeah," I frowned. "But what the fuck you mean '*no condom??*'"

"Nigga, I can't get pregnant in my ass – duh!"

"So?!? That ain't the only thing to worry about…"

"Nigga, what you tryna say?!?!" she snapped, feeling offended. "Shut the fuck up – don't act like you ain't slipped up and put it in without a condom before, either! Last two times you woke me up with it…what happened to the condom, then?"

"Yeah, but," I searched for the words to explain.

"Yeah, but *what*? You know I ain't fucking nobody else right now. Are you???"

"No," I lied with a straight face. "But still…"

"Still what???" she sat up on the bed and leaned towards me, as I was reaching in the pockets of my jeans. Standing on both knees…she reached down and put her fingers in her dripping wet pussy…getting them drenched. Without warning, she then grabbed my dick…wiping all her juices on it, "There. Now you got me all over you again. Fuck that shit."

This girl is crazy. But she's right. We had been fucking almost three months now and I went in raw twice on the late night. We always be drunk when we fuck so…shit happens. I'm just really particular about condoms and protected sex…I've been kid and disease free for this long for a reason. It's a hard *conscious* decision to make…one that I've never been able to make with a chick that wasn't my girl. I mean – on the contrary…I've been fucking with Cookie off and on for almost three YEARS…and we *always* use a condom. KeLLy was my main chick for the last two years…and up until our recent breakup…she was the only chick I would have raw sex with. Even *we* wear condoms now if we have sex…which is very rare over the last two months. For the most part…I've only been fucking Tianna on the regular now.

She's staring at me right now, and it's like she can read my mind and see what I'm contemplating.

"What you scared of?" she asked innocently.

"Shit…everything, bitch."

113

"Don't be. You can trust me," she promised. Here…you know what…"

"What?" I shot her a curious look.

"I'll look for my test papers. They around here somewhere. I gotta get tested for my job anyway," she rambled. "Nigga, I ain't got shit. I don't play like that."

I take a big gulp of gin, "Well, look for 'em, then…"

"Ugggghhhh, you get on my nerves!!!!" she hopped off the bed in frustration…and slapped my hard dick. It jumped back at her and she giggled.

"You play too much…"

"I'm too drunk and horny for this right now, dude," she started going through some papers on the dresser. There's a stream of juices running down her leg on her inner right thigh. She's not lying about the horny rage.

"Me, too, though," I looked down at my stiffness.

"Where the fuck did I put that shit at?" she whispered to herself.

I kept sipping my drink and jacking my dick as she searched. The longer she looked…the more tipsy I got and the less I gave a fuck. Whatever she got…if she got anything…I done already hit it raw twice. It's too late, anyway.

114

Maaaaan…I've gotta stop thinking with my dick one of these days.

Tonight ain't that night, though…

I walked up behind her…dick poking her in the crack of her ass, "Aye…come on."

"Nah, lemme find this shit so I ain't gotta hear yo punk ass mouth, nigga…"

"Fuck it…it's cool," I reassured her. "Get up on the bed."

She turned around to face me…licking her tongue out. She so fucking sexy when she being slutty like this. I grabbed her by the neck with my left hand…and slapped her face twice with my right – not hard, but just enough to piss her off. And when Tianna is pissed…she gets even more slutty and whore-ish.

Minutes later…she's in the bed on her back, and I'm on top of her…biting and licking her nipples as she fingers her pussy. She keeps grabbing my dick…rubbing my head against her pussy lips. I wanna shove it in her so bad…but I told her if I fuck her in the ass with no condom…she gets no pussy penetration 'til next time. The *KY Warming* lube is on the side of her left cheek in the bed with us.

"Ok," she mumbled in between breaths. "I think I'm ready…"

115

"You sure???"

"Yeah," she paused. "*GO SLOW,* nigga…for real. Don't play."

"I'm not. I got you," I gave her my word.

"I'm serious," she replied nervously. "You go too fast and I'ma bite yo ear off."

"I believe you, too. Just relax. I got you Tee…"

I sat up and told her to hold her legs up as I started pouring the lube on my **wooD.** Soon as I started rubbing it in…it started to activate and my dick felt like I had it wrapped in a warm towel. She watches my every move…biting her lip. After I got my shaft lubed up…I started rubbing her asshole with my index finger…slowly sticking it in. Her ass muscles immediately tightened up around my finger…almost pushing me out.

"Go slow…hmmm…ok," she moaned and squirmed. "Yeah…like that. Stick another finger in."

I obeyed her request…digging two fingers in now…going extra slow and steady – trying to see how far I could get 'em in. Her asshole was tight…tight as fuck. I don't know how my dick is supposed to fit. I mean…I'm no Mandingo…let's be clear. But a dick is a dick….and this is gonna be an extra tight fit.

She's gonna need more lube. And relaxation.

116

I dove headfirst into her pussy...not taking this part slow at all. I put her whole pussy in my mouth, trying to suck the fatness out that muthafucka while I kept fingering her ass. For the most part, I just kept my fingers inside without moving them...letting her ass muscles get used to the insertion.

She started humping my mouth and grinding against my fingers...hot with anticipation, "Shit...that feels so...*damn!* You *know* you can eat some pussy, boy!! Gotdammit!!!"

While she was in the usual amazement at my mouth skills...I pulled my fingers out her asshole. It was throbbing and clenching in front of me...ready.

The head is always the hardest part. If you can get the head in...the rest is less of a challenge. Soon as I rubbed it against her asshole...her pussy started cumming. Moving and grinding her hips with excitement...Tianna then grabbed my dick and started helping me slide it in....

It's *sooooo*...fucking...*TIGHT*.

I got my dick halfway in...and she put her hand on my chest...stopping me. I slapped her hand to the side and my weight fell on her – so now she couldn't push me away. I reached down and grabbed my dick at the base and balls...and started forcing it in further.

"Oooooowwwwwwww......*shit!!*" she gasped. "Ok. Ok. Ok, ok, ok, ok...wait. Dammit, boy."

117

"You ok???" my dick was throbbing inside her ass and I was about 5 inches deep now.

She's breathing hard. And *loud*. I've never heard her breathe this loud.

"Yeah…I think so," she tried to brace herself. "Shit. Nigga, yo dick don't seem that damn big. Fuck."

I let out a laugh, "I mean…it's yo ass, baby. I told you." I started thrusting while I talked shit.

"Whoa! Hold up, nigga! I said…go…slow!! Shit," she winced. "Yeah…like that. Slow down…"

"I'm barely moving Tee Tee…"

"Fuck!" she sounded surprised. "Ok. Ok…come on."

I sat up and grabbed her legs underneath her kneecaps to hold her down in place. I'm looking down at my dick in her ass…dripping with *KY*. I still don't see how it fit…but it's in there now.

I started thrusting slowly…still barely moving. It was more of a grind…digging and poking…trying to get it all in. If I woulda pulled back too much…she woulda pushed me out, for sure. Now that I was finally in there…I ain't want that. She was squirming and running a little bit, so I had to chase her. By the time she crawled all the way to the headboard I realized now she couldn't go anywhere else.

I pin her down.

And now I'm really in it. Working it…stroking it.

She's taking it now…reaching up to put her hands around my neck. I followed suit and started choking her while she took my fully erect dick. The whole scene made me drool on her tits like a baby.

She's in heaven. She starts fucking me back. Her ass was really open now and I was giving her forceful strokes. She's cussing at me…calling me all types of shit. Screaming at me…telling me how she hates me. This bitch was crazy. But all crazy hoes got good sex…and Tianna was no different.

I can't believe I'm doing this shit!!! I can't believe that this **hooKup** *done turned into* **this**.

In that moment, I made a silent promise to thank the person who hooked me up with Tianna tomorrow morning, cuz it can't get no better than this.

This is just what I needed after **KeLLy's Revenge** *– just what I needed to get my mojo back and get back on my 1-2.*

I can feel all the tension and frustration getting released. All the emotion and feelings wrapped up in KeLLy and Cookie…all the times I've **cheated** and got my creep on…all of my sexual experiences and fantasies – all of it was running through me in this moment. It was an amazing feeling of redemption and conquest. At that very moment, I felt more alive than ever before.

I forget I'm in her ass and I start ramming and pounding. I can't even hear her objections anymore...I pay no attention to her scratching and clawing at me. She's swinging on me – but not pushing me out. She loves the abuse. Tianna is the type of chick who thrives on getting mistreated....and who am I to disappoint?

I grabbed the back of her neck...and lifted her head up so she could watch my dick going in and out of her ass. So she could see what type of nasty shit she had me doing right now.

This makes both of us reach that point. She can feel my dick swelling up...ready to let go, "Oh my...*God*...you bout to cum, baby???"

I can't even talk right now...

"Huh, baby?" she keeps moaning. Come...on. Gimme...gimme dat dick...you better...oh my – *fuuuuuck...*"

Her cursing and incomplete sentences were working wonders for my ego. I'm in a drunken rage now – sweating and dripping all over her, giving her hard strokes of recklessness.

"You better...cum! Better cum...in...my...oh my God! Baby, please cum in my ass! I wanna feel it..."

It's THROBBING...JUMPING....

"Fuck," I stopped stroking.

"Yeah baby? Come on...hmmmmmmmmmm shit!!!" Tianna screamed loudly. "I feel it...I feel it baby!!!! Oh my gaw...it's so warm...oh my *GOD!!*"

She looked at me in confusion, but I knew she wuttin' confused. She knew exactly what was going on...she asked for it.

I'm shooting a huge load now...and I can feel the cum dripping out of her ass and back on my dick, "Hmmmmm. *Fuuuuuuuck*...gotdammit, girl!!!"

"Let it out, baby...yes! Let that shit...*OUT!!*"

Her ass muscles were squeezing it out of me as she looked at me and bit her lip in passion.

She's so sexy...little China doll looking ass bitch.

Soon as the last drop was out, I pulled out of her ass and we fell on top of each other...again.

"Get off me, nasty ass nigga," she said in disgust.

"Fuck you. Freaky bitch."

*   *   *   *   *

The next morning is where it gets crazy.

I leave Tianna's house around 10:30 am...wore out

121

as usual.

Once I was in the car and on the highway…I remembered that I needed to make that '*thank you*' phone call. I've gotta thank the nigga who hooked me up with Tianna….and let him know how this shit has been working out. We've hooked each other up many-a-time over the years…but this last **hooKup** was one for the record books.

I'm a grateful-type nigga…so I always gotta remember to give thanks.

I picked up my phone and dialed my homeboy *Tre's* cell, "Yo nigga…I'm on my way! You ain't gon' believe what the fuck just happened, bro."

"Nigga, don't say I ain't never hooked you up, nigga!" Tre talked shit as usual. "I told you dat lil bitch was a freak, nigga!"

"I know…you did" I gave him his props. "This bitch is a super freak tho, cuzz! You ain't tell me she like getting fucked in the ass, nigga!"

Tre started laughing hysterically, "Nigga, you know I ain't with all that kinky shit, nigga! See, that's why I had to pass her to you, my nigga – I leave all dat kinky shit to you, Ro."

"Fuck you, nigga," I had to laugh at that. "I ain't got no shame."

"Damn, nigga…you put it in her booty??? See, man these hoes out here ain't shit!"

"She wanted it, bro!" I insisted. "She said *Tyrone* wuttin' giving her what she want!"

"That bitch really think my name is '*Tyrone*', too. *Dumb ass bitch.* How far are you, bro?"

"I'll be there in like seven minutes nigga. I'll call you when I'm outside."

"Bet."

    *   *   *   *   *

10

So, when I pulled up...I popped my trunk and grabbed my change of underwear and basketball shoes. I always kept extra underwear in the ride. You never know when you might have to take an emergency shower.

Especially now that I was back in KC and running the streets with Tre again. This nigga kept me on my toes when it came to the pussy chase...he was a different type of dude.

Tre and I had been close friends since we were 16, and now – 9 years later – we were as close as ever. We hung out every chance we got and, just like brothers, we shared everything. Secrets...tips...stories...women.

Well not *all* women.

Just those bitches who didn't mean much...the hoes that didn't matter.

*   *   *   *   *

Tre was being a real friend when I called him after **KeLLy's Revenge** and told him I was moving back to KC and would need some new hoes. Normally we would hit the clubs and the parks up...but it was the end of December and bitches like to stay in when it's cold. In the wintertime – chicks are chose up, already got dey cuddle buddy to keep 'em warm all season. So, when I told Tre I needed a little freak bitch, he had the perfect idea.

There was this chick he had been fucking with for a minute...and he was growing tired of her. For him it was just fucking. For her, as usual, she was falling for his ass. Tre was never the kind of nigga to get too emotional or serious with a chick....it was all fun and games with him. But because it was such a game, he was also the type of nigga to not tell a bitch the truth about the situation. If the bitch caught feelings...that was on her. Tre could care less about a bitch with hurt feelings...my nigga was just heartless like that. So much to the point that he was willing to let a bitch think the dynamics of their relationship was more than what it truly was. I mean...the nigga had been using 'Tyrone' as a fake name for chicks since we graduated high school.

So...in the case of Tianna...like always, Tre led this bitch on and had her really believing things were getting serious. I mean – the nigga went and had Thanksgiving dinner with her family! He admitted that he was starting to feel the pressure after Thanksgiving, and she was talking less about sex and more about a commitment. So, once I called him about my need for new hoes...Tre figured the best way to get rid of the bitch was to make the bitch forget about him.

That's where I came in. The plan was simple…and though it sounded like a long shot, we put our heads together and made it work.

First, we agreed that she needed to get a changeup…after dealing with a nigga like Tre. Me and Tre were a lot alike in some ways and our lingo and vocabulary got intertwined, so it was going to be a challenge for me not to remind her of Tre. I needed to be like a knight in shining armor…like the complete opposite of what she was used to. And under no circumstances could we let let her find out we actually knew each other…that might get us both cut.

Tre had met her off *BlackPlanet*…and said that they just started chatting with *Inbox* messages before he ended up fucking her a week later. He fucked her the first night they met so he said it should be no different with me. And like most females who are freaks…they be closeted about it, so the other strategy was to not push up on her. Tre said she'a give me the pussy with no hesitation if I just played it cool like he knew I would. Tre didn't have no chill…he had no idea what playing it cool was. So, if *he* was able to come out of there with the pussy, he was absolutely sure I would be as successful.

The last thing I needed to remember was that the bitch loved to get drunk, and once she had liquor in her…she'd be down for whatever. One last warning Tre had for me was the fact that she was a *biter*. One of the reasons Tre was ready to get rid of her…Tre wasn't into that kinky shit.

My first contact with Tianna was a random *BlackPlanet* message:

THE_KUMFORT-HER: *"Hey wassup stranger..."*

SEXYMISST816: *"Stranger? Do I know you?*

THE_KUMFORT-HER: *"Oh it's like that now? You don't remember me?"*

SEXYMISST816: *"Uhm no I don't know you."*

THE_KUMFORT-HER: *"We met at Roadhouse last summer when I was home for break. We was talking for a lil minute before I went back to school. You don't remember?"*

SEXYMISST816: *"Nope. Last summer?"*

THE_KUMFORT-HER: *"Yup, before I went back to school. We hung out once, don't you stay out in Grandview with your Mom and little brother? You don't remember we went bowling at Loma Vista?"*

SEXYMISST816: *"Hahaha dang how you know that? Yeah but I'm bout to move to my own spot next weekend. You wanna help me move? Lol."*

THE_KUMFORT-HER: *"Lol if I'm off I will. I'm back home now, I graduated."*

SEXYMISST816: *"Aww that's sweet, but I was just playing. Congrats tho."*

THE_KUMFORT-HER: *"Not being sweet...just being me. But I do wanna hang out with you again or something now that I'm back."*

SEXYMISST816: *"I don't remember us hanging out though. You don't look familiar in your picture, it's kinda blurry."*

THE_KUMFORT-HER: *"I mean it was a while ago, it's January now. Don't be talking about my pic, that's yo dial-up internet lol! Your pic is hella small too, look who's talking!"*

SEXYMISST816: *"Forget you! I gotta learn how to work this scanner! People be saying they can't even see my face smh."*

THE_KUMFORT-HER: *"LOL yeah you can't! I remember what you look like though, you got that sexy ass mole and pretty eyes. I'll never forget that."*

129

SEXYMISST816: *"Damn. Maybe you do know me! I don't remember though, that's crazy. So are you working now that you graduated?"*

THE_KUMFORT-HER: *"Yeah, I'm in training now. You?"*

SEXYMISST816: *"I work in home health. So where is your girlfriend at?"*

THE_KUMFORT-HER: *"I'm single. Just got out of a relationship...not looking for one really. Just wanna meet friends and have fun."*

SEXYMISST816: *"Aww I'm sorry. Me too. Relationships are for the birds."*

THE_KUMFORT-HER: *"I agree. But we should still hang out, or talk off of here. You down?"*

SEXYMISST816: *"Uhm...you're not a stalker or anything right? Lol people be crazy on the internet!"*

THE_KUMFORT-HER: *"No I'm not! Lol! And we met at the club, so technically I'm not an internet date!"*

SEXYMISST816: **"Lol ok ok that's right! You silly!"**

THE_KUMFORT-HER: **"Ok so can I call you later? What's your number?"**

The rest was history. She never knew what hit her.

*　　　*　　　*　　　*　　　*

When Tre opened the door, he had his phone in his hand with the biggest grin on his face.

"What's so funny, hoe ass nigga?" I raised my eyebrow.

"This *Lonnie* on speakerphone," Tre chuckled. "I was just telling him how the bitch had you tied up, fucking you with a dildo!"

"Yeah right, you fag ass nigga! Fuck you!"

Lonnie was cracking up on the other end of the phone, "Nigga I still can't believe you let that hoe tie you up. You lose some points for that, dawg."

"Oh well, she ain't tying me up no more!" I told the homies. "I be over there hogging that bitch out dog...real talk."

"Nigga, whatever," Tre dismissed me. "I bet I can still fuck!"

"Only cuz you called the bitch fucking with her emotions n'shit, nigga!!!" I called Tre out for his bullshit.

Tre tripped up the stairs, dropping his phone on the steps he was laughing so hard. I picked it up as I walked past him and up the stairs to the bedroom, "Aye Lonnie, dis nigga calls the bitch acting like his feelings hurt cuz she done moved on! Just on some childish shit!!!"

"Man, you know dat nigga ain't got no sense," Lonnie reminded me.

"Bro, dis bitch almost was feeling bad for him! He had her thinking he was gon kick her door in n'shit!!!"

"Aye, nigga fuck that bitch!" Tre exclaimed. "I had to play dat shit like it was real, dawg. Shit…this nigga Ro being all nice to the bitch, making love to her n'shit!!"

"Yeah right, nigga," I flipped him off. "I fucks her like a porn star."

"So bro…dis bitch really don't know y'all know each other, dawg?" Lonnie wanted to understand. "How???"

"Lonnie, dawg…she ain't never seen us together," Tre explained. "Ro been in the Burg n'shit…he wuttin' out here like me and you!"

132

"Yeah, but the bitch always ask me if I know you…she thought we knew each other at first, dawg. You know how we talk alike n'shit, I had to keep playing it off like dis shit crazy…"

"Man, y'all niggaz both crazy, bro," Lonnie almost sounded embarrassed.

"Aye…my nigga said he needed some new hoes… and what *Tre* do?" Tre was proud of his antics. "*Tre* said '*here…have my hoe.*' Real nigga for you."

"Yeah, yeah, whatever, nigga…that hoe just being a hoe," I looked down at the phone. "Aye, hold on Lonnie. This nigga phone clicking."

I hand Tre his cell and he takes a look at the *caller ID*, "Nigga, I don't know who number that is…it ain't saved."

"So, nigga??" I screwed my face.

"Answer it for me, bro. Keep it on speaker…just say hello."

Reluctantly, I hit the *TALK* button to click over, "Hello???"

SILENCE.

I look at Tre…who was being quiet as hell, trying to see who's on the other end.

"Hellllooooooooooo????" I repeated.

The female voice on the other end was angry, "Who is this?!?!"

"Uhm…who is *this*? You called me," I smirked.

"Yeah…I called. But I didn't call *you!!!* Who is *THIS?!?!?!*"

Tre and I look at each other…eyes both wide.

It's *Tianna.*

SHIT. OH. *SHIT!!!!!*

I hang up the phone quickly and Tre and I just stare at each other for a minute.

"Damn bro…what the fuck???"

"Damn, dawg, I ain't know that was her, bro!" Tre couldn't believe it. "What number is that she calling from???"

"Fuck, nigga! She supposed to get her house phone cut on today," I suddenly remembered. "I bet that's what it wa…"

Just then *my* phone rings. Now she's calling me.

"Shit. Bro, she calling me now…fuck! I ain't gon' answer."

I let it ring for what seems like it forever.

RING….

….**RING**…

……**RING**…

Finally, it stops. But then she just calls *right* back.

I looked at Tre nervously, shaking my head, "Damn, bro. I gotta answer."

*　　*　　*　　*　　*

11

I walked over to a chair next to Tre's bedroom closet and sat down. He was sitting still as hell at the computer as I answered.

"Hello?"

"Nigga, where *you* at???" Tianna snapped. "I just called you twice."

"My phone was in the other room," I lied. "Wassup??"

"Nigga...where are you at?!?! You with *Tyrone!!!*"

"Huh? What are you talking about?" I tried to sound confused. "I'm at home..."

"You lying!" she screamed. "I know yo voice! I just called his phone from my house phone and *you* answered!!!"

"Girl, you are crazy," I chuckled, playing it smooth.

"Nah, nigga...I ain't crazy!" Tianna wasn't fooled. "I know what I just heard!"

Her voice was high-pitched through the phone, and she was obviously fighting mad.

This is dat BULLSHIT!!!

"Girl, I don't know what the hell you talking about."

"So, why it take you so long to answer? *And* I called you twice!"

"Maaan, I just said my phone was in the other room, girl! You tripping...for real, dude."

"No, I'm *not!*" she yelled. "Just be real, Rodney! You telling me you don't know who I'm talking about?"

"I have no idea," I chose my tone carefully, trying not to set her off any further.

"You lying!!! Oh my *God* – both of y'all are some *liars!!!* I swear...niggaz ain't about shit!!!"

"Man, ain't nobody got time for this shit, man. I'm 'bout to hang up on you."

Tianna started spazzing, "You better not fucking hang up on me, nigga! I swear to *GOD* – don't hang up on me, boy! You caught – just man up and admit it!"

Tre was looking at me, shaking his head in disbelief. This bitch done pulled some slick shit...on *accident.* I'm just sitting there in shock...jaw dropped. I can't believe it.

Out of all of the things...after all this time...

"HELLO?!?!?!" she blurted out.

"Yeah, I'm still here," I replied quietly. "You wilding out right now."

"Oh my *God* – no I'm *not*, nigga!!!" she screamed excitedly. "I know yo damn voice by now!! I know what I heard – you not 'bout to make it out like I'm crazy! That was *you!!!*"

"How was it me when you on the phone with me now?" I tried to deflect. "That don't even make sense!"

"Yeah, well that's what I'm trying to figure out. I think I know," she paused, voice drifting. "Hmmm…yeah, I think I got a good idea what's going on."

"What's going on, Tee?" I challenged her.

I don't even know why I'm asking…maybe she doesn't have it figured out. I mean…ain't no way she could know everything at this point…it's impossible. The least she may have figured out is that me and *'Tyrone'* know each other.

But still…I gotta at least *try* to save face. This bitch is crazy…ain't no telling what her ass is thinking right now. Ain't no telling what this sick bitch might do.

Like right now…she's quiet as fuck.

"Hello?" I checked to see if she was still there.

"Yep," at the same time she speaks, I hear Tre's phone ring again behind me.

Heart skipping a beat…I immediately freeze up as he fumbles with the phone for a second before silencing the ringer.

139

SHE KNOWS.

Oh shit.

"Whose phone is that ringing, Rodney?!?!?!" she yelled. *See,* nigga?!? That's *Tyrone!* I'm calling him now! Y'all niggaz are caught!!!"

"Maaaan, what? That was my lil cousin walking outside," I kept lying. "I don't know what you talking about Tee Tee. You tripping…"

"Man, see I shoulda *knew* y'all niggaz knew each other – that shit was just *too* fucking ironi…."

"Man, what the fuck are you talking about, man?!?" I yelled back angrily at her, trying to steal the momentum. "I'm at home – I don't know no *Tyrone!*"

"Fuck you, nigga! I fucking hate y'all niggas!!!" she hung up in my face.

I could feel her fury all the way in Tre's bedroom.

"What she say, bro??" he asked anxiously. "She know it was you? Deny that shit, nigga!"

"Maaaan…she know, bro," I admitted. "I mean, she don't *know*…but she KNOW, nigga. She know my voice. We thew, nigga."

"Man, fuck that hoe, nigga. She don't know shit, dumb ass broad."

"Bro, and then you ain't answer yo phone when she

called you!!!" I complained. "Damn, nigga!"

"Nigga, I ain't know what to do!" Tre argued. "Why the fuck dat bitch calling me from a unknown number, anyway??? I'm 'bout to call dat bitch back and cuss her out."

"Nah bro...don't do that" I pleaded. "Lemme call her."

"And say what, nigga?" Tre wanted to know my intentions. "You 'bout to *apologize* to the bitch?"

"Hell nah, nigga. I'ma just try to calm her down – you know you gon' say something to piss her off! Have her out here looking for our cars n'shit!!!"

"Nigga, I wish dat bitch *would* fuck with my car," he smirked. "You the one gotta worry...yo dumb ass told the bitch ya real name! Sucka ass nigga!!!"

I laughed him off, "You a hooooooooeeeeeee!!! Damn, dawg. Dat bitch don't know where I live, though. And I'm 'bout to move out next month anyway nigga."

"Yeah, nigga dat's right. You should be cool, then. Fuck that hoe. You might as well move back in with KeLLy now, though, nigga."

"I should, huh?" I thought about it. "I don't know, nigga. Man...fuck. Dat bitch had some good pussy too though, my nigga..."

"Nigga, you can fuck her again...all you gotta do is call her," Tre suggested. "Just let her cool off. She gon need some more dick, nigga. Watch what I tell you."

"She was maaad, though, bro. If I call her, I can't admit that shit."

"Nigga, if you don't call her, I am," Tre threatened. "I wanna fuck that bitch again, too…shit. You talking bout she swallowing nut n'shit, nigga!! Bitch ain't never swallow my cum!!"

"Nigga, cuz I get kinky with the hoes, nigga. You be on that regular shit."

"I ain't gotta do all that shit, nigga," he bragged. "I fucks better than you, nigga!"

"Yeah right, whatever nigga!" I flipped him off.

"Aye! We can call Tee Tee right now and ask her! Where my phone at???"

"Nah, nigga…don't do that, bro!!!"

Tre laughed, "See, look at you! Feeling sorry for dat hoe!! Fuck her, nigga!!!"

"I'm just *saying*," I ignored his nonsense. "Lemme call her first…play damage control."

"Aight, nigga. I'ma give you two weeks to fuck her again and then Tyrone gon call," he warned me.

I didn't expect nothing less coming from this nigga Tre. Laughing, I agreed to his challenge, "Aight, nigga. That's a bet."

*   *   *   *   *

Tre and I decided to cancel our basketball game at State Line and I told him I'd keep him posted before I headed back to the crib. Soon as I pulled up at my aunt's, I called Tianna.

She answered on the first ring, "What, nigga?"

"Why you acting like that?" I asked softly. "What I do to you???"

"You ready to stop lying now?" she asked me sarcastically.

"Lying about what, baby?"

"See, nigga you wanna keep playing!" she yelled. "So, how long y'all been knowing each other? This *whole* time???"

"Tee Tee…I promise I don't know what you talking about," I insisted. "I don't know what you think you heard…but you ain't heard me with ole boy. Think about it. How does that even make sense?"

"It makes perfect sense to me cuz I know what I heard. I'm crazy. But not that crazy, nigga."

"So you think me and ya ex been knowing each other the whole time?" I made it sound ridiculous. "Who does that? Like what would be the point?"

"Niggaz do shit like that all the time," Tianna was convinced. "Y'all niggaz on some slick shit."

"Man, you is *tripping*! Real talk, dude," I stuck to my story. "That wuttin' *me* whenever you get through. You had the wrong number or something. You tripping!"

"So you really sitting here telling me that wuttin' you that answered his phone? Nigga. I know yo voice!"

"I'm saying this nigga got you bugging, whoever it is. Like...you for real tripping out."

"Even if he do got me tripping...I know that was you, Rodney. I know it was."

"So why would I be calling you now?" I asked her. "If I'm so-called friends with this Tyrone nigga?"

"I don't know, nigga," she confessed. "Being a nigga. Trying to play the shit off. See...he ain't know my new number, that's how y'all got caught up."

"Nah, man. I ain't got time for no games like that. I told you I just got out of a relationship before I met you. I'm not for that kind of drama. You got me mixed up. I....am not him. Now maybe yo last nigga was into shit like that, but I'm on some grown man shit. You tripping, ma."

"Maaaan...I don't know," she held her ground. "I just...I know that was you. It sounded just like you. It damn sure wuttin' him that answered."

144

"Well, it wuttin' me. But I mean...what the fuck you calling him for *anyway*?" I changed the subject. "I thought you was done with the nigga."

"I mean I was just calling him," she tried to explain. "I felt bad. I don't know. I was just checking on his ass."

"Sound like you missing the nigga for real," I accused her, knowing she'd get triggered.

"Whatever! Fuck him! For real. I mean...it don't even matter for real. Niggaz ain't shit."

"Don't be putting me in that box, though," I requested. "I ain't done shit to you..."

"Nigga you, too!!" she refused to give me a pass. "You ain't *shit*. Whether it was you or not...you still ain't *shit*. You just got good sex...that's it."

"Damn, that's fucked up."

"I'm just being honest. Something *you* niggaz can't do these days."

"So that's all I'm good for?" I asked for clarification.

"You got some good dick. I'll give you that. Him too, shit. That's one thing I can't take from y'all. But whatever."

"You just gon keep putting me in a box with this hoe ass nigga..."

145

"Ok fine – whatever – it wasn't you!" she finally gave up. "I don't even give a fuck no more! For real! If it was it was…oh well. We already fucked now."

"So what you saying? You done fucking with me??" I bit my lip.

"Hmmmm," Tianna thought about it. "I should be."

"But…???"

"But nothing. I don't know. I'm pissed off right now for real, so don't be asking me no shit like that right now."

"You want me to call back and ask in fifteen minutes???"

"Fuck you, nigga!!" she snapped at me.

"Fuck *you*."

"Oooooo, you get on my muthafuckin nerves, nigga!" she was breaking down. "Cute ass nigga. Fuck you."

"You wanna be mad at me so bad…but it's *that* nigga you mad at."

"What do you know, nigga?"

"I know you need to forget about that nigga. I know I help you not think about him."

146

"Whatever, boy."

"You know it's true. And you know you wanna see me again."

"So…?" she didn't deny it.

"So, you tell me," I lowered my voice.

Tianna paused for a second before answering. She was definitely more calm than when I first called…but she was still on the fence, "Maaan. If I find out that was really you…"

I cut her off, "Tee Tee…you bugging. This is *me* you talking to *now*, baby. This is Daddy."

"Ughhhh," she sighed in frustration.

"Stop acting like that. I wanna see you. Lemme come see you," I went in for the kill.

"No."

"Tee Tee…"

She smacked her lips, "When?"

"Later on. I'ma call you when I'm 'bout to be on my way."

"Ok, punk ass nigga," she cursed at me.

147

"Fuck you, *bitch*. I'll call you later."

"Ok. Bring dat lube back, you bastard."

*   *   *   *   *

It was fun while it lasted. I mean – I had some damn *good* times with Tee Tee. And, if nothing else, now that I think about it, I gotta give Tianna her proper credit for helping unleash the BEAST that's grown so much stronger since then. I only fucked her twice more after that day…and then I made a decision to lock the beast back in the cage so Kells and I could give it another shot without distractions.

But *Tre* aka *TYRONE*??? He just couldn't leave well enough alone, and when I stepped out of the picture and had KeLLy move back in with me…he crept back in Tee Tee's life like I never even happened. He had to fuck that girl at least five more times after that – we sat around and laughed about it.

Tianna never brought it back up with me, but apparently the last time Tre beat it down, they got into a heated argument and he finally threw it in her face how she was stupid enough to let his homeboy fuck.

I know…I know. Niggaz ain't shit. For what it's worth, though, I did feel guilty after all'at. I mean, Tre and I went through a lot to fuck with this girl's mental state. And part of me was sure she knew it was me on the phone that day we got caught, anyway. But, at the same

148

time, she couldn't prove it yet. And my charm is no joke.

Let's be clear. ~~Beast~~ unleashed or not, Tianna never stood a chance fucking with a wolf in lamb's clothing like me.

But dealing with *TWO* **WOLVES** who run in the same pack??? Nigga. Now *that's* a real ***hooKup*** for yo ass!!!

No hard feelings, Tee Tee. It's all in name of the game...

FIN.
(Until We Cheat Again)

ABOUT THE AUTHOR

"HoLLyRod" – the author and creator of the highly controversial and raunchy storyline, *The Art of Cheating* – is the alter-ego and pseudonym for established writer Rodney L. Henderson Jr.

Since graduating with a Business Administration degree in Computer Information Systems from the *University of Central Missouri*, Henderson has showcased his writing skills in various forms of art – including radio commercials and music, as well as poetry and promo spots for fashion companies such as *DymeWear Inc* and *Ridikulus Kouture LLC*.

HoLLyRod's short story mini-series titled ***The Art of Cheating Episodes*** introduces readers to the many characters and mystery behind **HoLLyWorld** and *The Art of Cheating*, while chronicling the ups and downs of infidelity through experiences based on real life. The ongoing series has been re-released in a special Extended Author's Cut Edition.

AVAILABLE IN eBOOK and PAPERBACK FORMATS!!!
AUDIO BOOKS COMING SOON!!!

Henderson currently resides in his home state of Missouri and spends most of his time managing and writing for *Angela Marie Publishing, LLC* – a company named after his late mother.

The Art of Cheating Episodes is published under *Lurodica Stories*, an erotica division of the publishing company.

"I just want to continue to be inspired at the notion of making her proud and keep my promise to share my talents with the world."

www.HoLLyRods.com
www.facebook.com/TheArtOfCheating
www.twitter.com/TheCheatGods

Next up on
The Art of Cheating…

SEASON 1 — EPISODE 6:
Ménages

Things with Sashé are just…different. She's nothing like KeLLy…or even Cookie, the best mistress-to-date in HoLLyWorld. Sashé may be younger than his tenured flames, but she's got the same type of sexual appetite that speaks to the ~~beast~~ HoLLyRod has had brewing inside for years. Not only does Shay like girls…she's also down for ménages – a world that's only existed in HoLLy's mind for as long as he can think back. In this Season 1 Finale, HoLLyRod is faced with the task of finally getting over this lifelong wet dream…and turning this fantasy into a live, in-the-flesh reality for the ages. The closer he gets, the more he's reminded that everything comes with a cost. And nothing ever goes exactly as planned…especially when it comes to *The Art of Cheating*.

EXTENDED AUTHOR'S CUT EDITION
AVAILABLE NOW

Also by HoLLyRod

The Art of Cheating Episodes
(Extended Author's Cut Edition)

SEASON 1
Episode 1 - Sassy
Episode 2 – Hangover
Episode 3 - HoLLy BeLLigerence
Episode 4 - KeLLy's Revenge
Episode 5 - The HooKup
Episode 6 – Ménages

SEASON 2
Episode 1 - Cyber Pimpin' (**12/22/22**)
Episode 2 - Campus Record (**2/15/23**)
Episode 3 – A Date with Karma (**4/20/23**)
Episode 4 – The Wedding Party (**6/19/23**)
Episode 5 – HoLLy & Sug (**8/23/23**)

SEASON 3
(Spring 2024)

Angela Marie Publishing
Presents

WDFFIL EP1: Facing the Music

The OFFICIAL Soundtrack to The Art of Cheating Episodes

AVAILABLE ON ALL MUSIC PLATFORMS

DOWNLOAD OR STREAM NOW!!!!

https://distrokid.com/hyperfollow/hollyrod/wdffil-ep1-facing-the-music-4

Angela Marie Publishing, LLC. All rights reserved.

153

Made in the USA
Middletown, DE
29 July 2022

70216099R00106